W9-BYX-840

MORE PRAISE FOR BABYMOUSE!

"Sassy, smart . . .
Babymouse is here
to stay."
—The Horn Book Magazine

"Young readers
will happily
fall in line."
—Kirkus Reviews

"The brother-sister creative team hits the mark
with humor, sweetness, and characters so genuine
they can pass for real kids." —Booklist

"Babymouse is spunky, ambitious,
and, at times, a total dweeb."
—School Library Journal

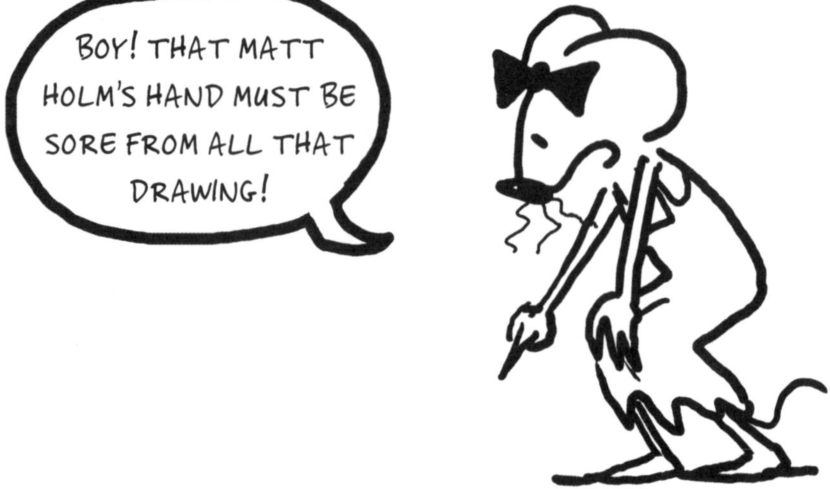
BOY! THAT MATT HOLM'S HAND MUST BE SORE FROM ALL THAT DRAWING!

Go fetch **all** the **BABYMOUSE** books:

#1 BABYMOUSE: Queen of the World!
#2 BABYMOUSE: Our Hero
#3 BABYMOUSE: Beach Babe
#4 BABYMOUSE: Rock Star
#5 BABYMOUSE: Heartbreaker
#6 CAMP BABYMOUSE
#7 BABYMOUSE: Skater Girl
#8 BABYMOUSE: Puppy Love
#9 BABYMOUSE: Monster Mash
#10 BABYMOUSE: The Musical

BABYMOUSE
PUPPY LOVE

BY JENNIFER L. HOLM & MATTHEW HOLM

RANDOM HOUSE NEW YORK

EWWW! NOT ON THE COPYRIGHT PAGE!

Copyright © 2007 by Jennifer Holm and Matthew Holm.

All rights reserved.
Published in the United States by Random House Children's Books, a division of Random House, Inc., New York.

RANDOM HOUSE and colophon are registered trademarks of Random House, Inc.

www.randomhouse.com/kids
www.babymouse.com

Educators and librarians, for a variety of teaching tools, visit us at
www.randomhouse.com/teachers

Library of Congress Cataloging-in-Publication Data
Holm, Jennifer L.
Babymouse : puppy love / by Jennifer & Matthew Holm.
  p. cm. — (Babymouse ; 8)
ISBN: 978-0-375-83990-0 (trade) — ISBN: 978-0-375-93990-7 (lib. bdg.)
I. Graphic novels.
I. Holm, Matthew. II. Title. III. Title: Puppy love.
PN6727.H592B325 2007
741.5973—dc22
2007061012

13 ᵈᵒᵍ

PRINTED IN MALAYSIA   15 14 13 12 11 10 9 8 7

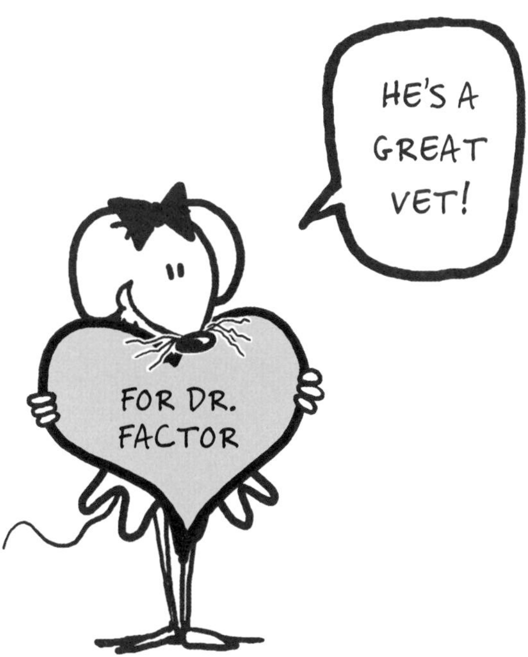
HE'S A GREAT VET!
FOR DR. FACTOR

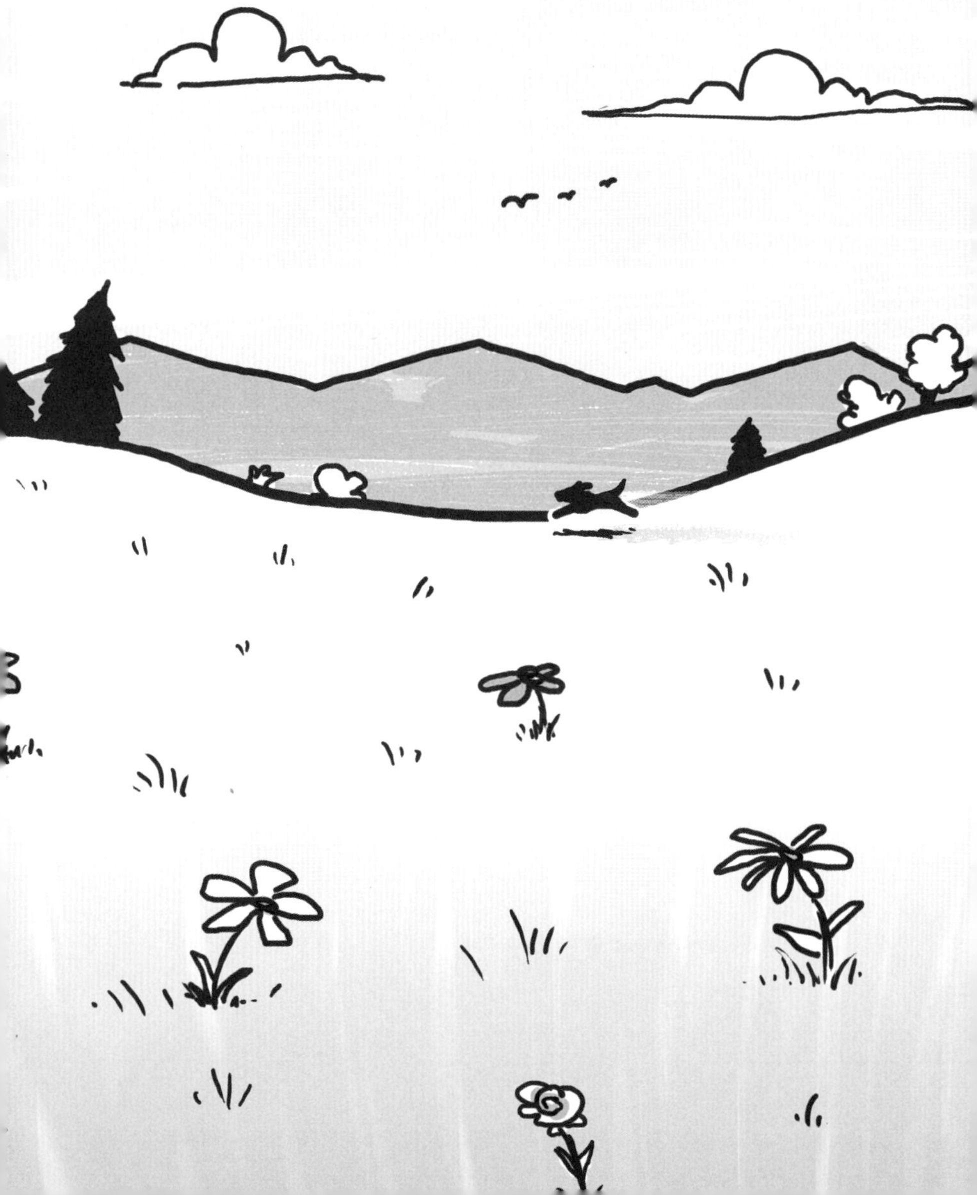

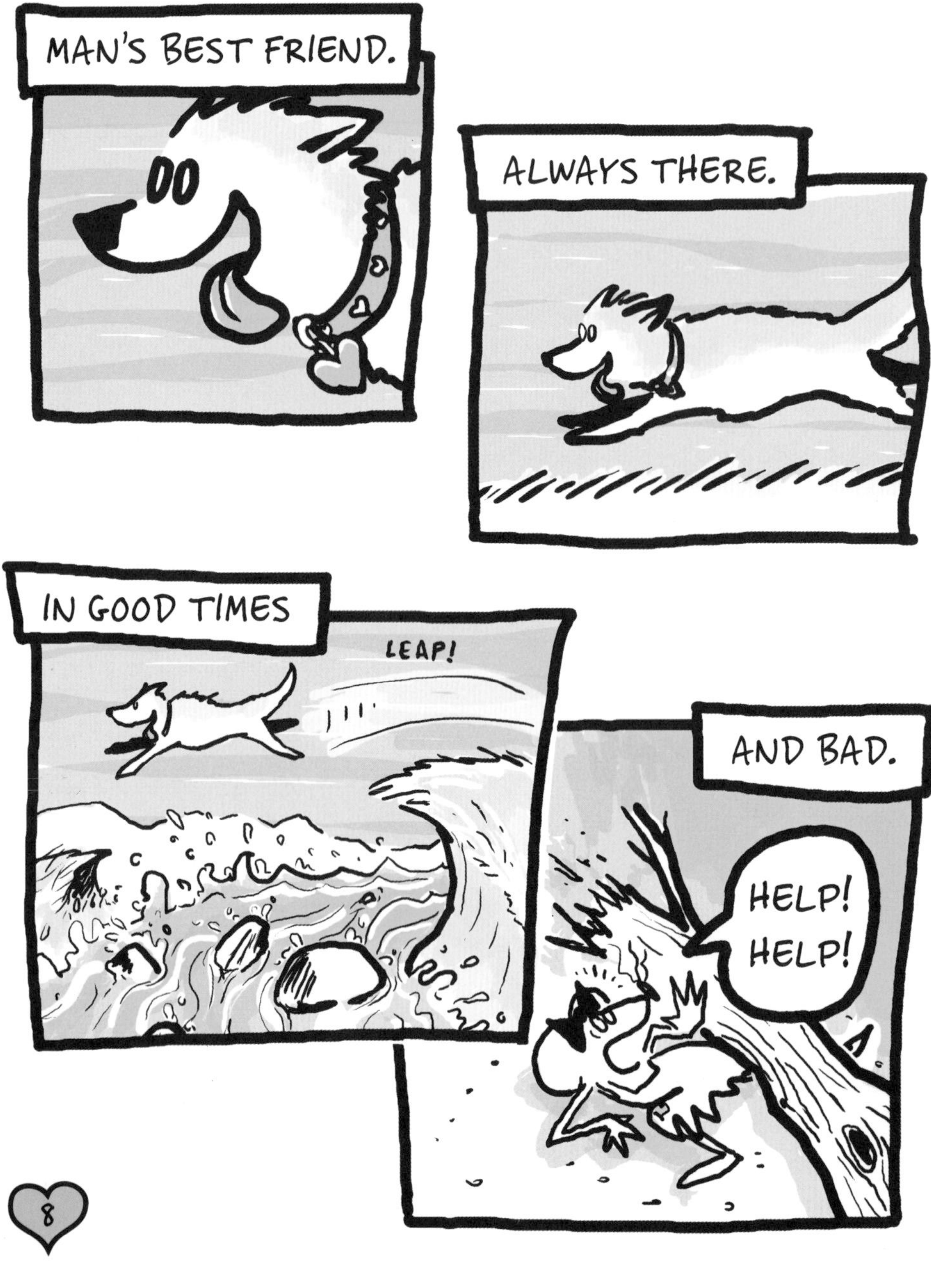
MAN'S BEST FRIEND.
ALWAYS THERE.
IN GOOD TIMES
LEAP!
AND BAD.
HELP! HELP!

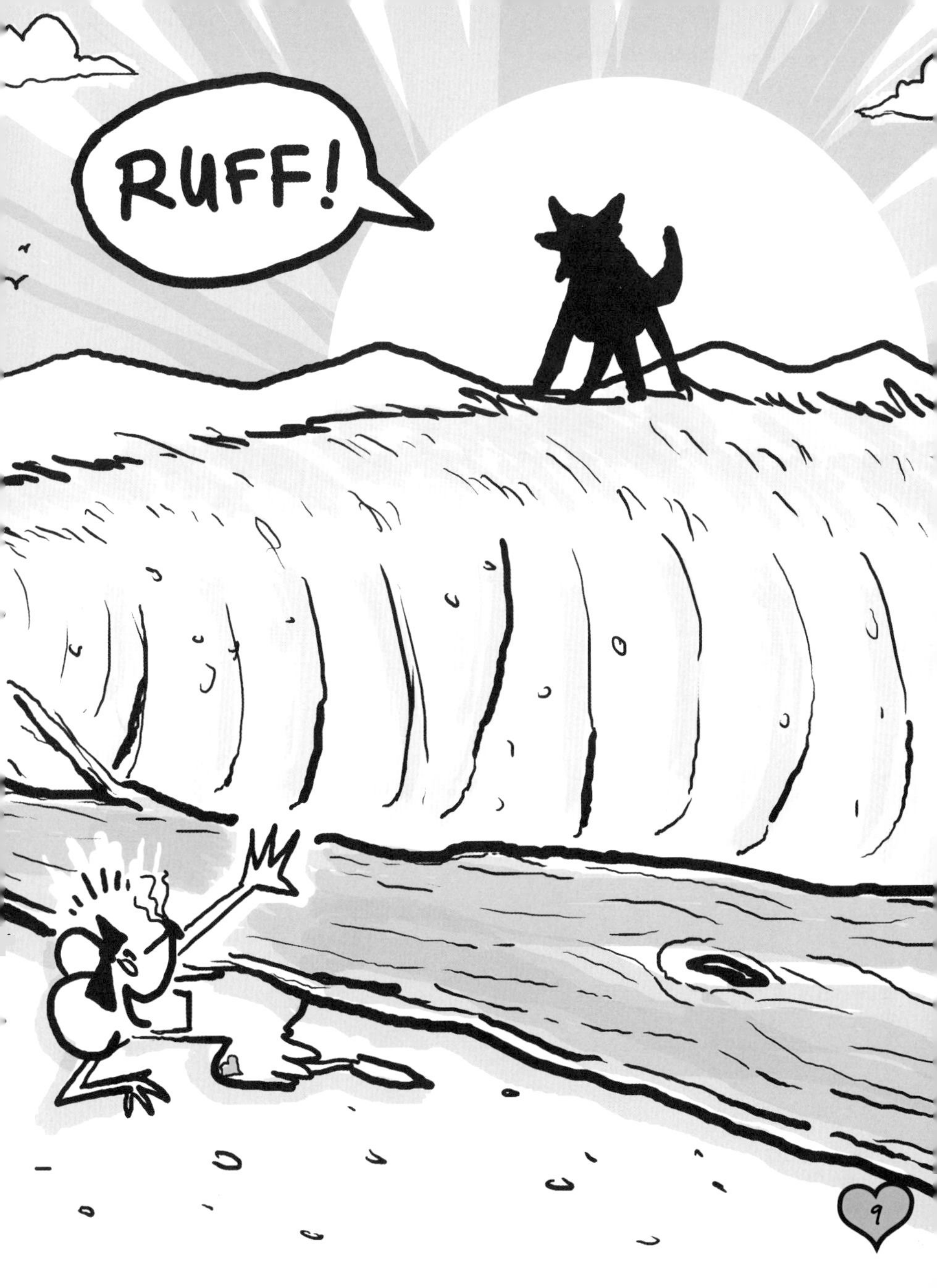
RUFF!

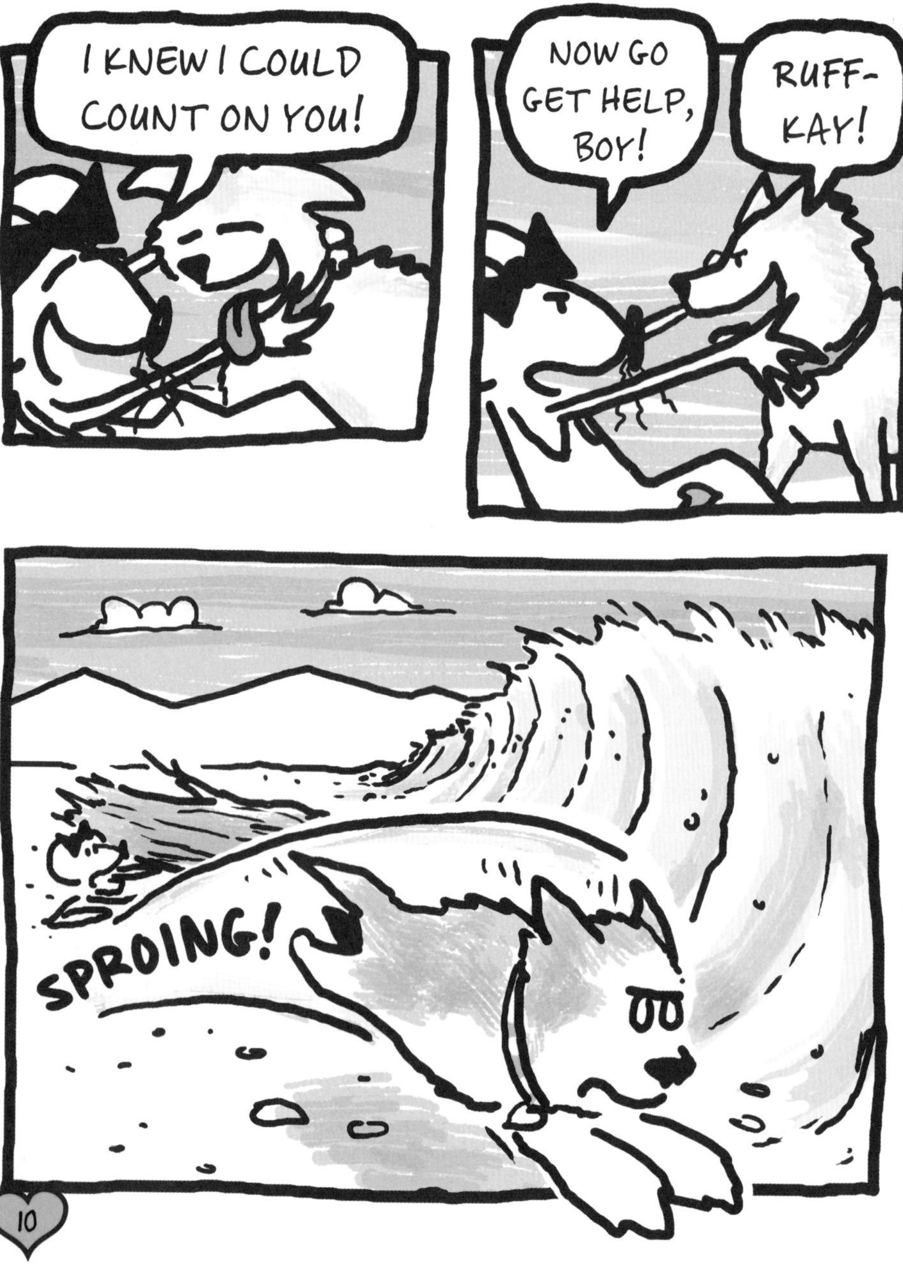
I KNEW I COULD COUNT ON YOU!
NOW GO GET HELP, BOY!
RUFF-KAY!
SPROING!

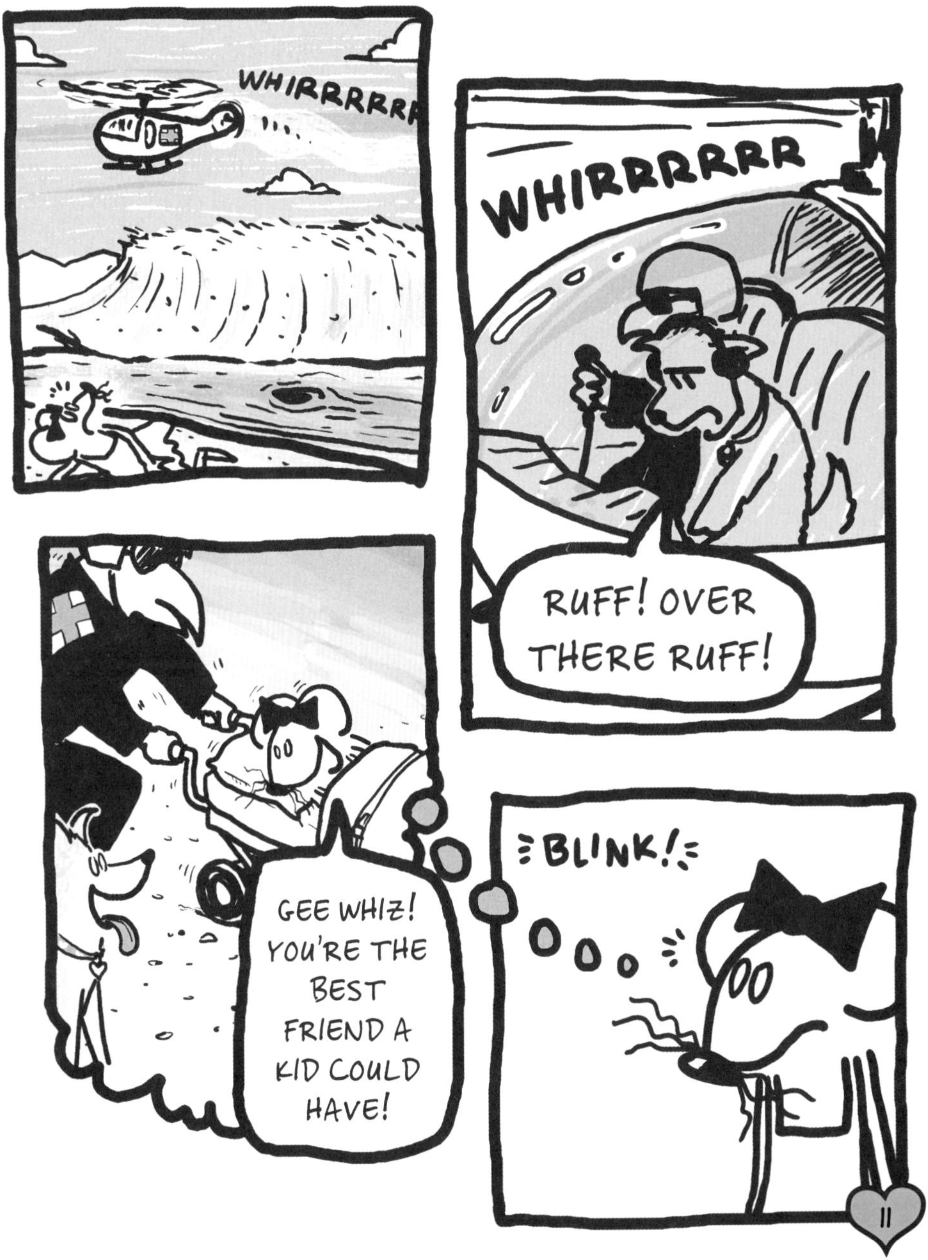
WHIRRRRRR
WHIRRRRRR
RUFF! OVER THERE RUFF!
GEE WHIZ! YOU'RE THE BEST FRIEND A KID COULD HAVE!
BLINK!

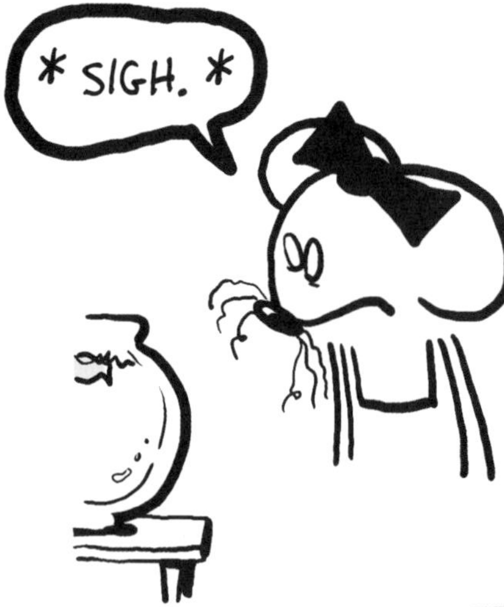
* SIGH. *

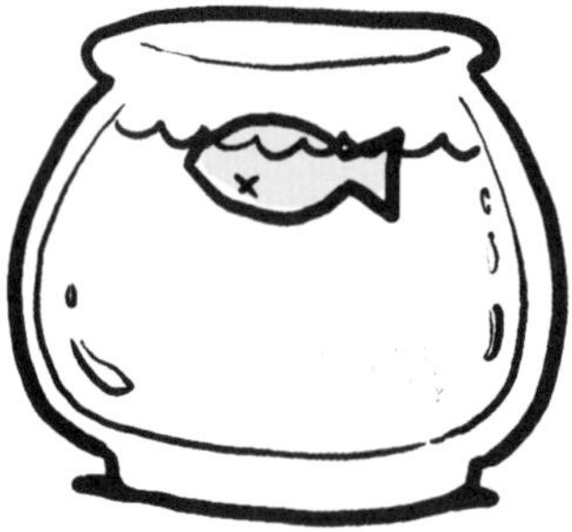

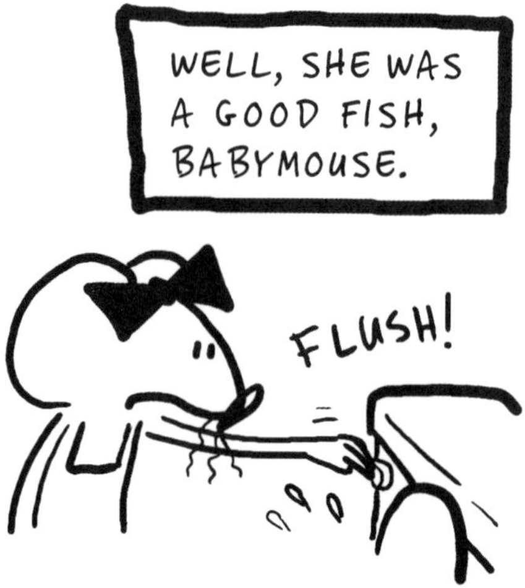
WELL, SHE WAS A GOOD FISH, BABYMOUSE.
FLUSH!

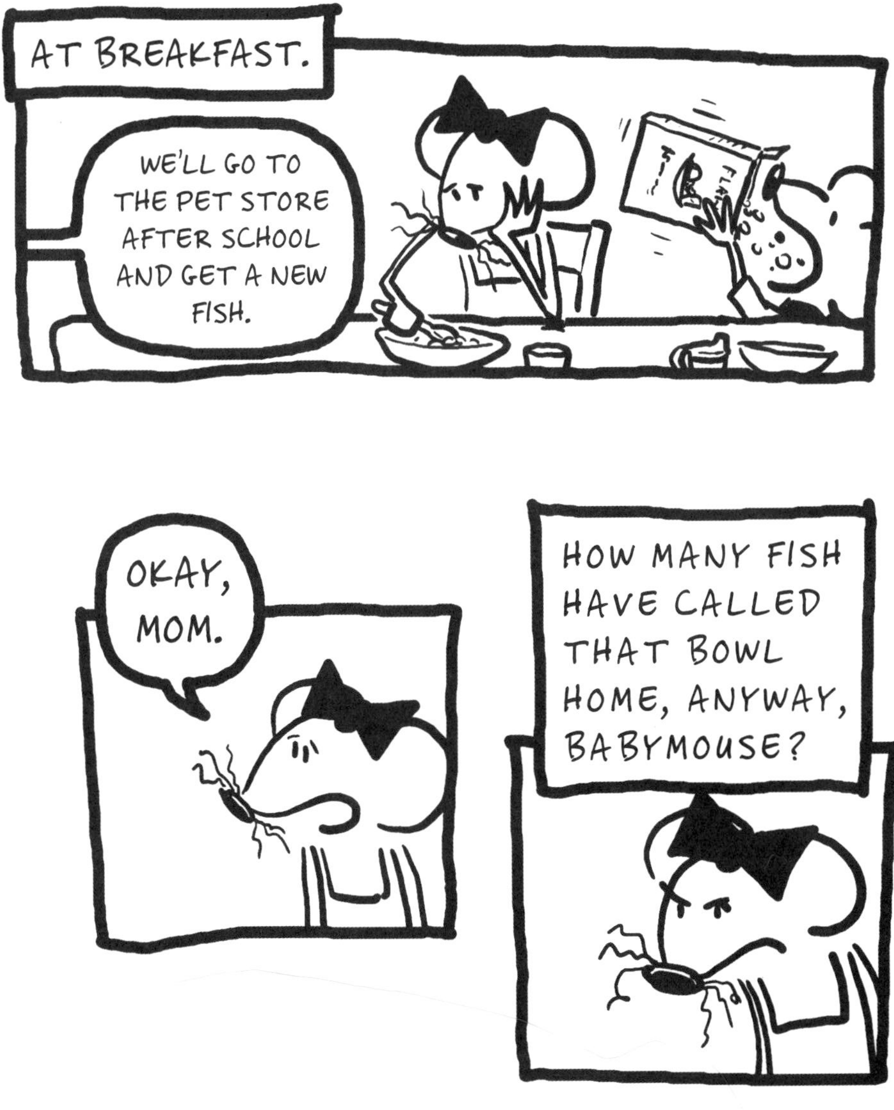
AT BREAKFAST.
WE'LL GO TO THE PET STORE AFTER SCHOOL AND GET A NEW FISH.
OKAY, MOM.
HOW MANY FISH HAVE CALLED THAT BOWL HOME, ANYWAY, BABYMOUSE?

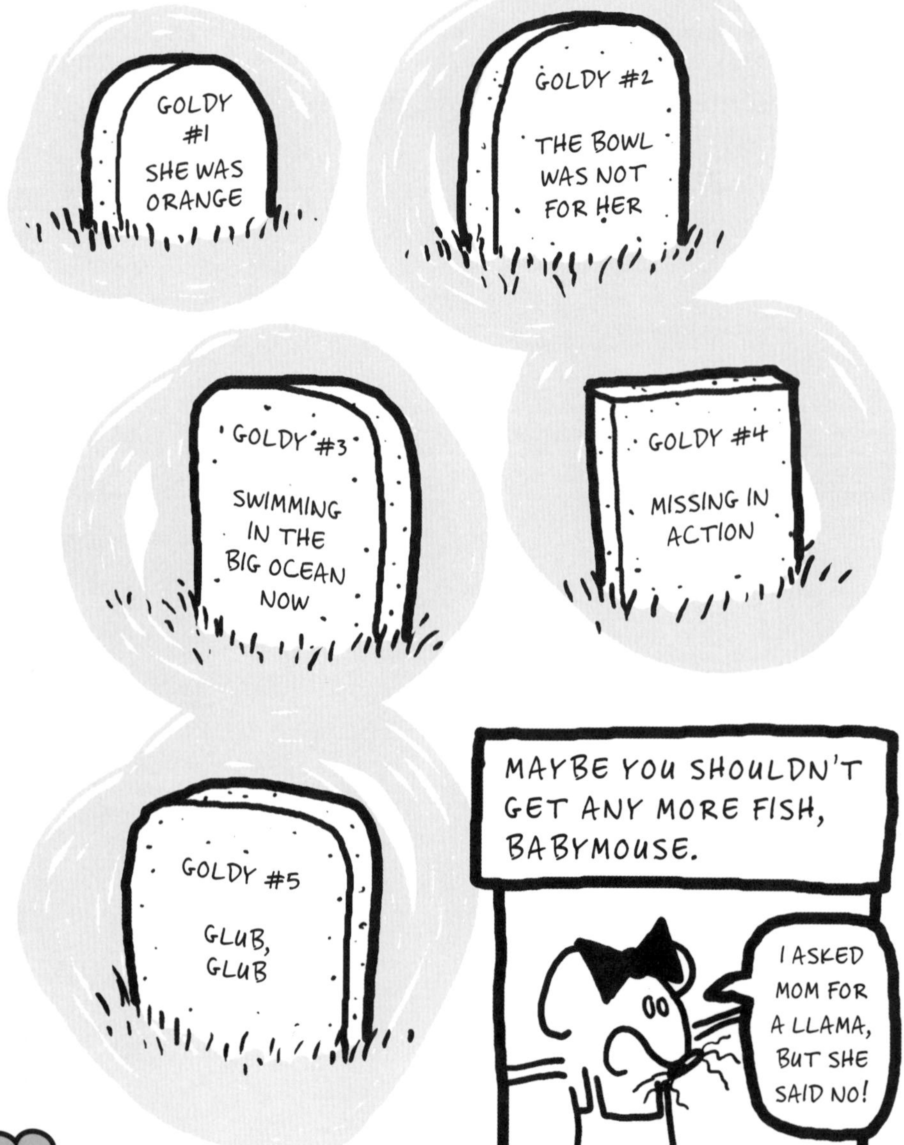
GOLDY #1 SHE WAS ORANGE
GOLDY #2 THE BOWL WAS NOT FOR HER
GOLDY #3 SWIMMING IN THE BIG OCEAN NOW
GOLDY #4 MISSING IN ACTION
GOLDY #5 GLUB, GLUB
MAYBE YOU SHOULDN'T GET ANY MORE FISH, BABYMOUSE.
I ASKED MOM FOR A LLAMA, BUT SHE SAID NO!

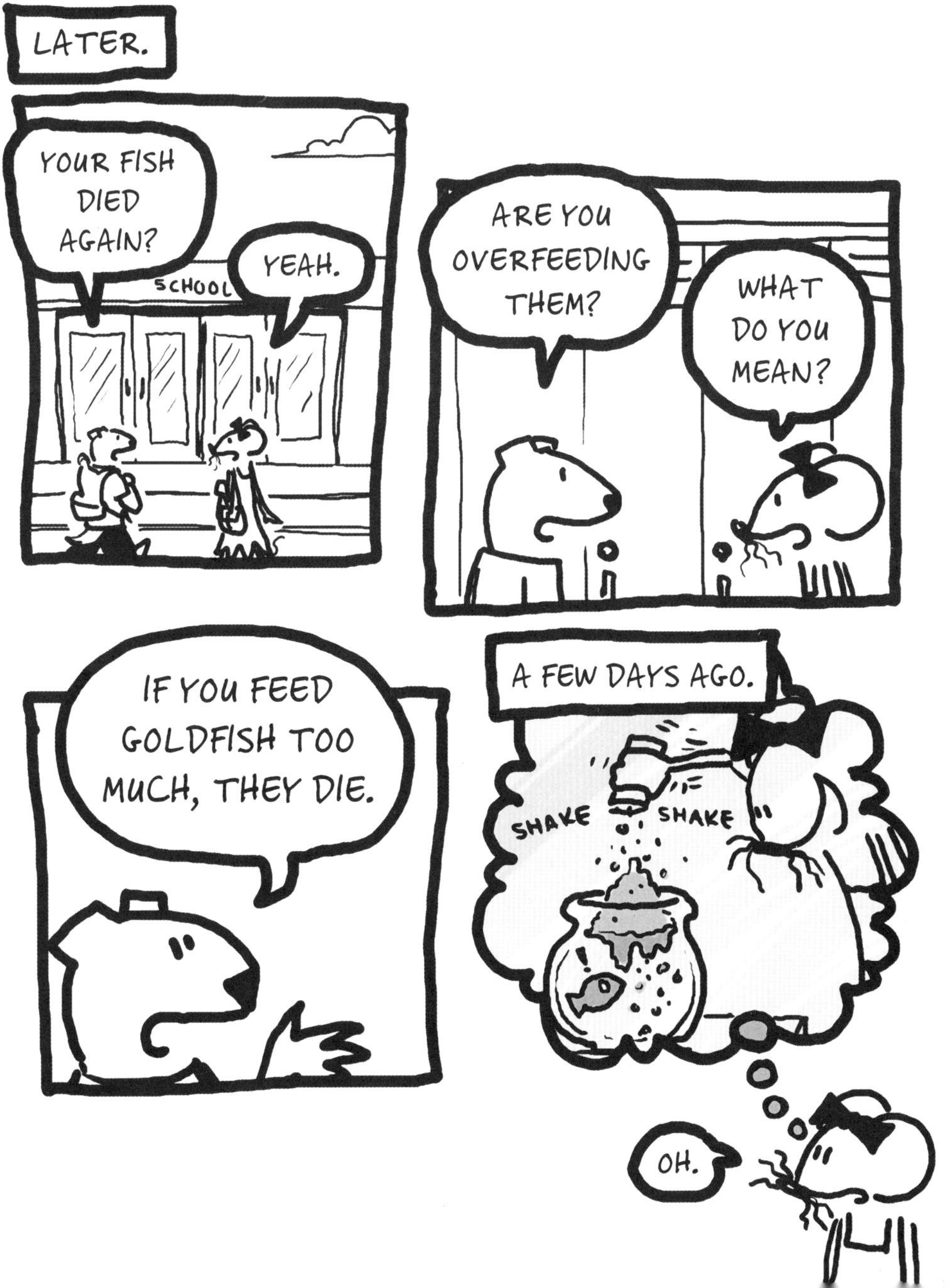
LATER.
YOUR FISH DIED AGAIN?
YEAH.
SCHOOL
ARE YOU OVERFEEDING THEM?
WHAT DO YOU MEAN?
IF YOU FEED GOLDFISH TOO MUCH, THEY DIE.
A FEW DAYS AGO.
SHAKE
SHAKE
OH.

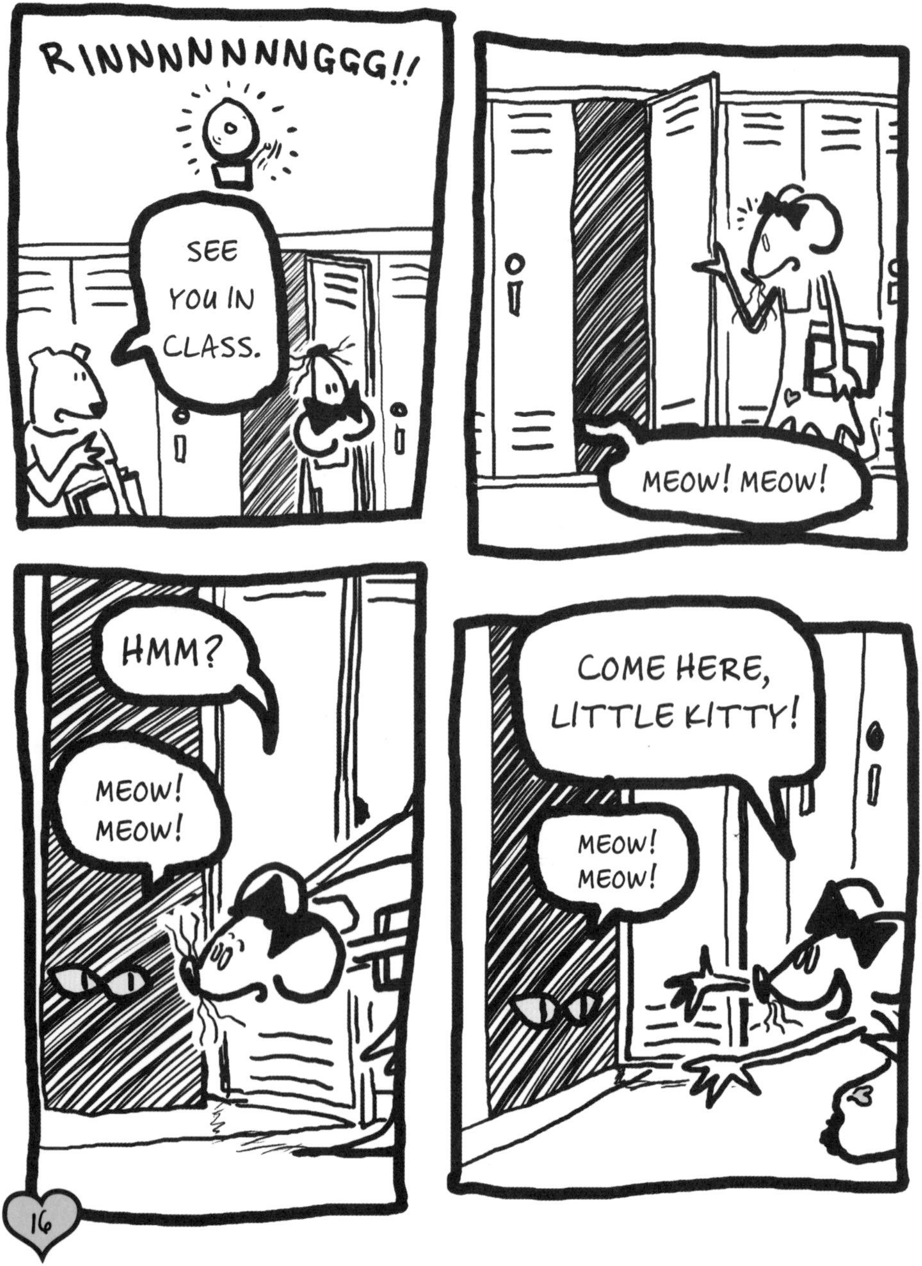
RINNNNNNNGGG!!
SEE YOU IN CLASS.
MEOW! MEOW!
HMM?
MEOW! MEOW!
COME HERE, LITTLE KITTY!
MEOW! MEOW!

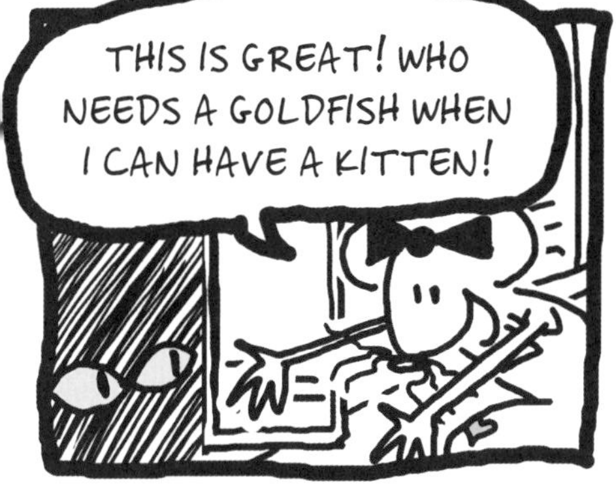
THIS IS GREAT! WHO NEEDS A GOLDFISH WHEN I CAN HAVE A KITTEN!

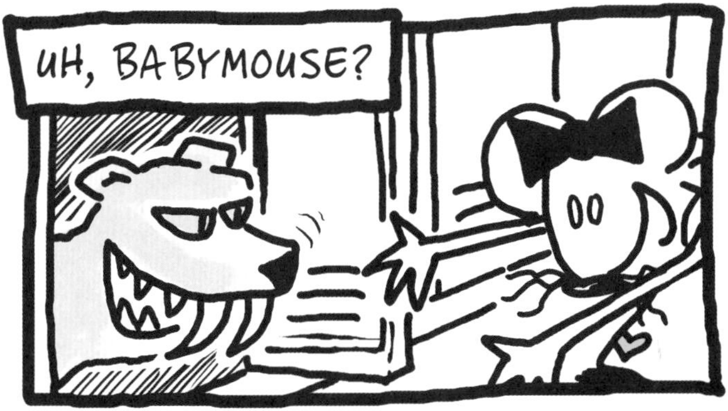
UH, BABYMOUSE?

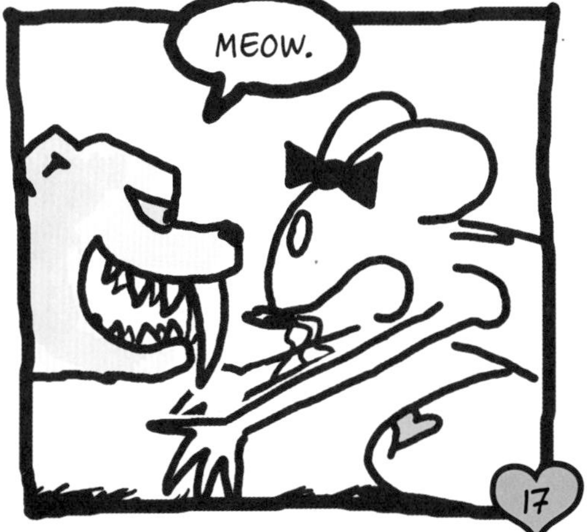
MEOW.

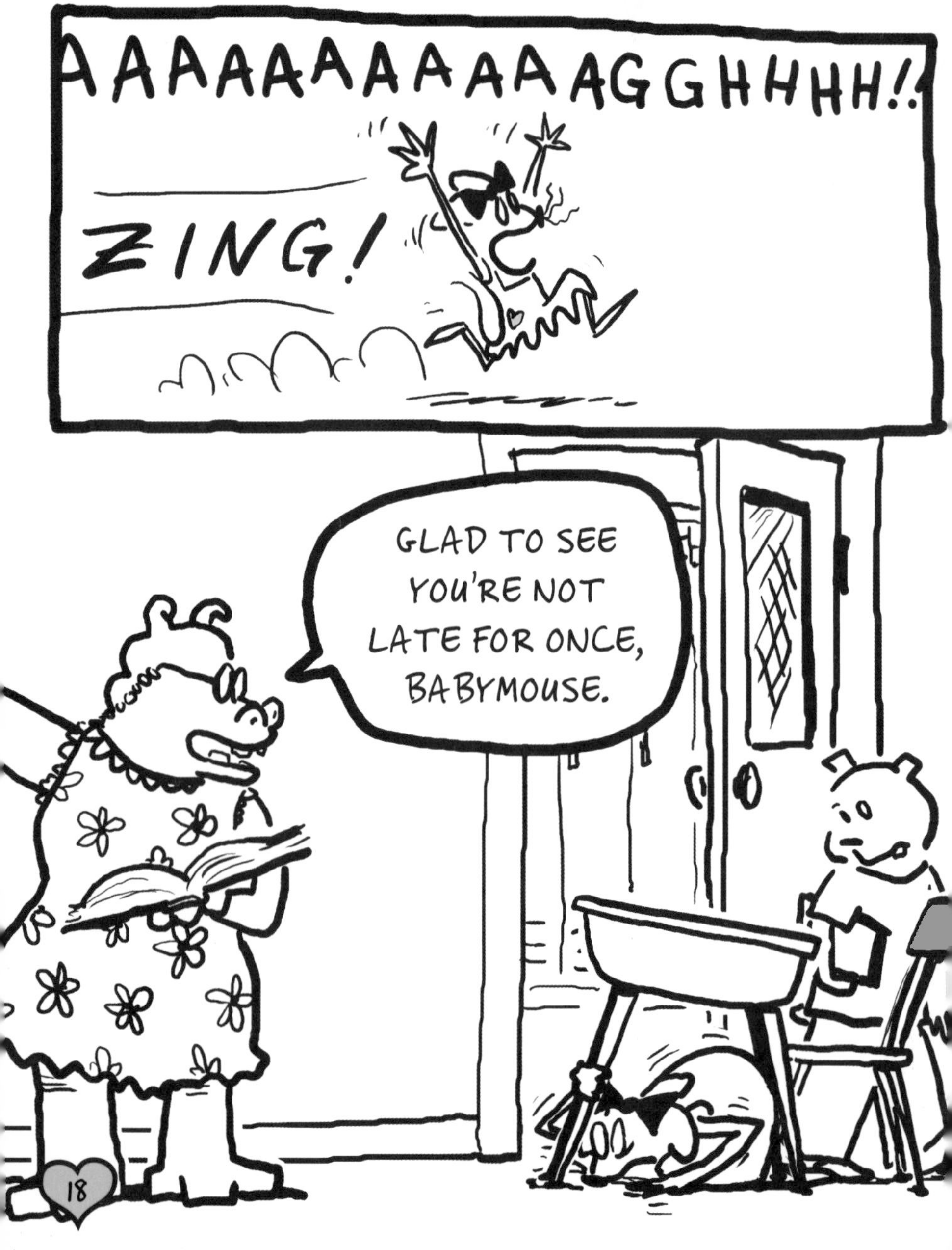
AAAAAAAAAAAGGHHHH!!
ZING!
GLAD TO SEE YOU'RE NOT LATE FOR ONCE, BABYMOUSE.

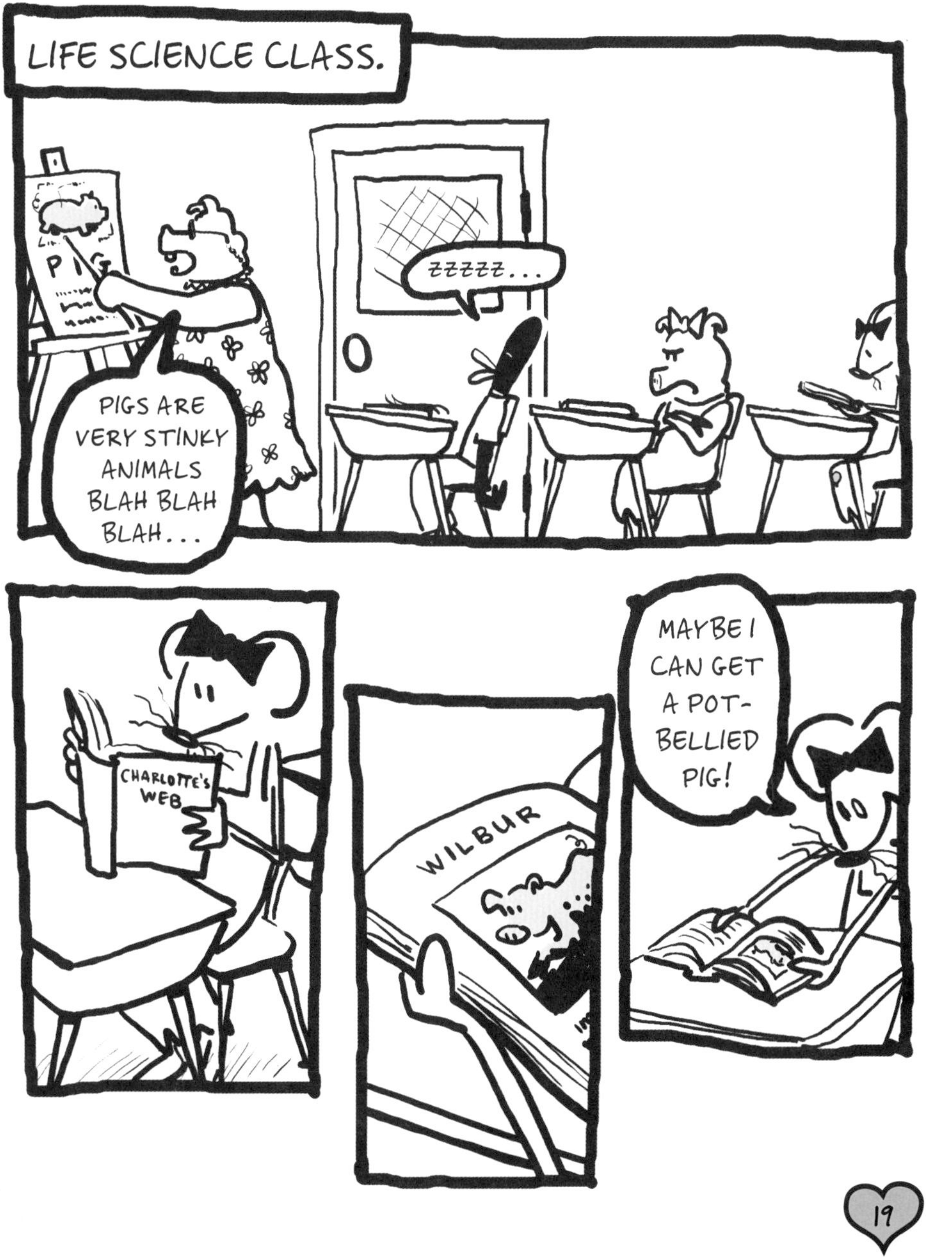
LIFE SCIENCE CLASS.
PIGS ARE VERY STINKY ANIMALS BLAH BLAH BLAH...
ZZZZZ...
P I G
CHARLOTTE'S WEB
WILBUR
MAYBE I CAN GET A POT-BELLIED PIG!

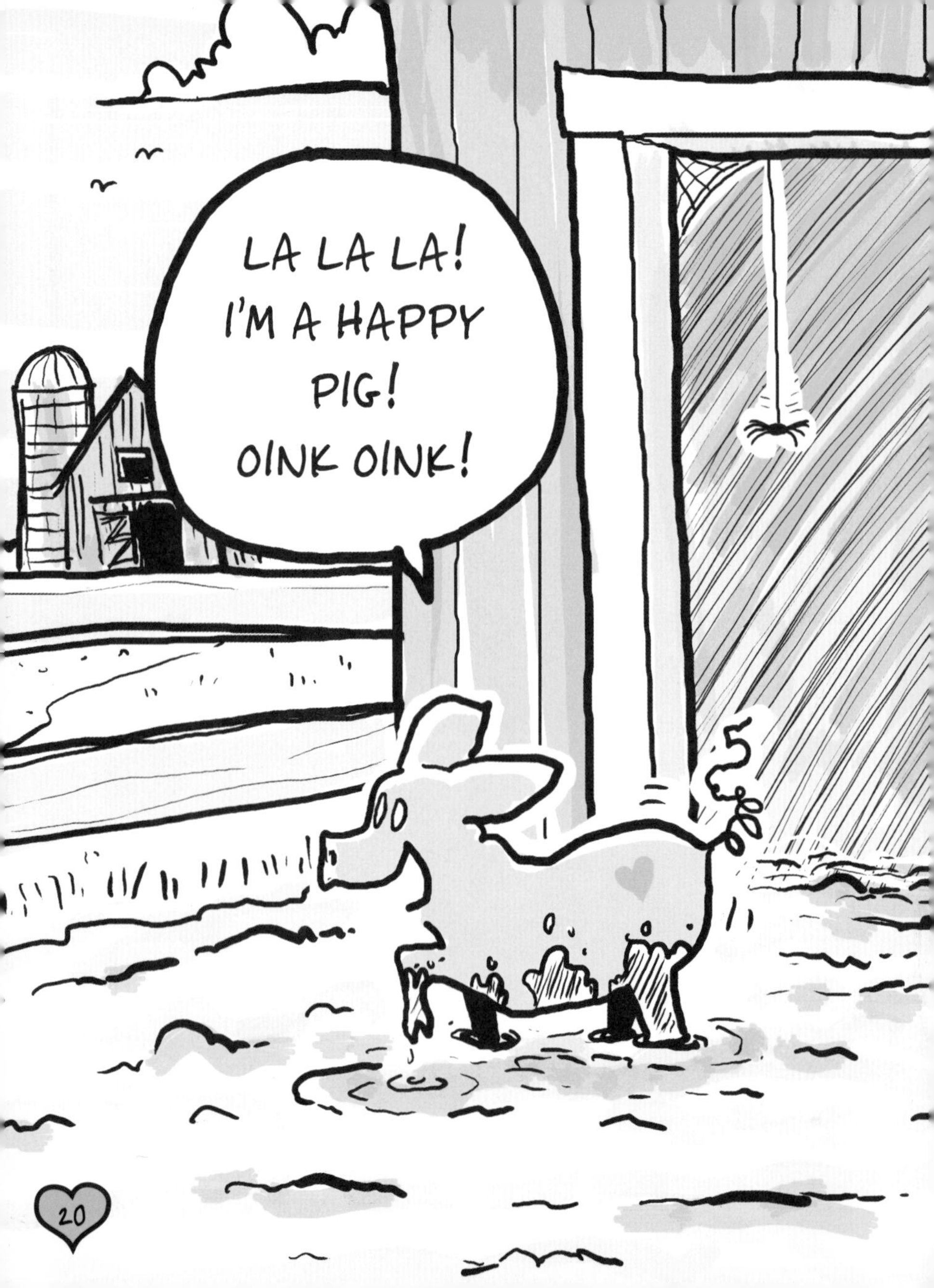
LA LA LA! I'M A HAPPY PIG! OINK OINK!

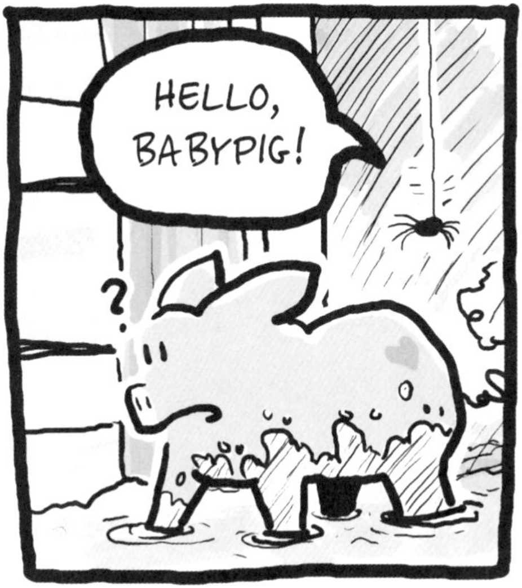
HELLO, BABYPIG!
?
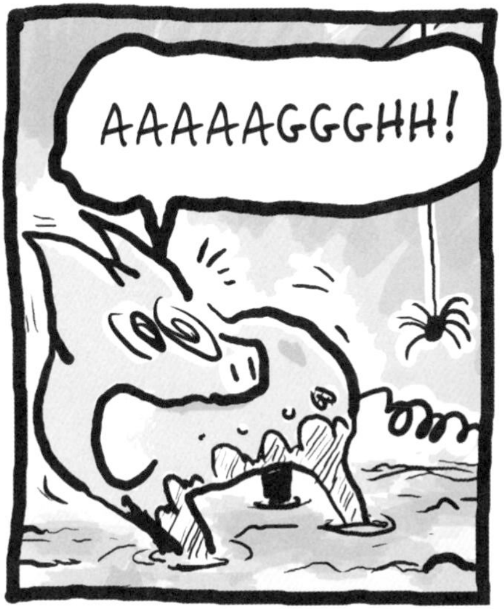
AAAAAGGGHH!
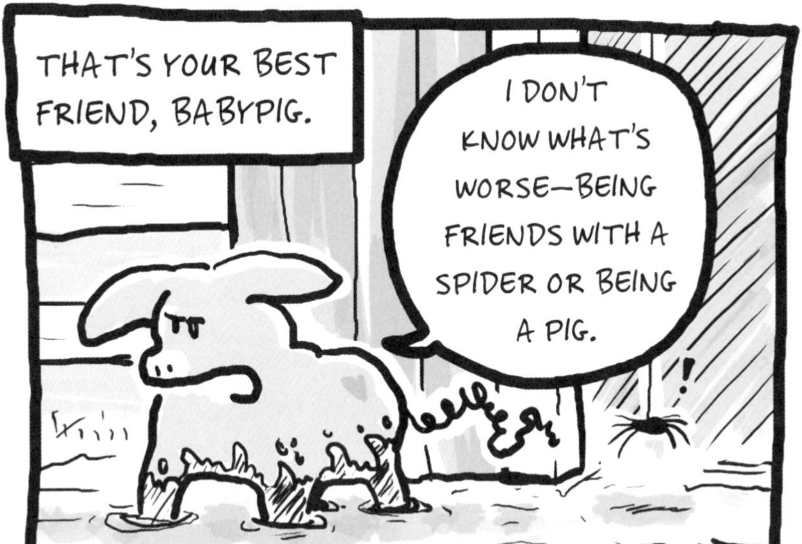
THAT'S YOUR BEST FRIEND, BABYPIG.
I DON'T KNOW WHAT'S WORSE—BEING FRIENDS WITH A SPIDER OR BEING A PIG.
!

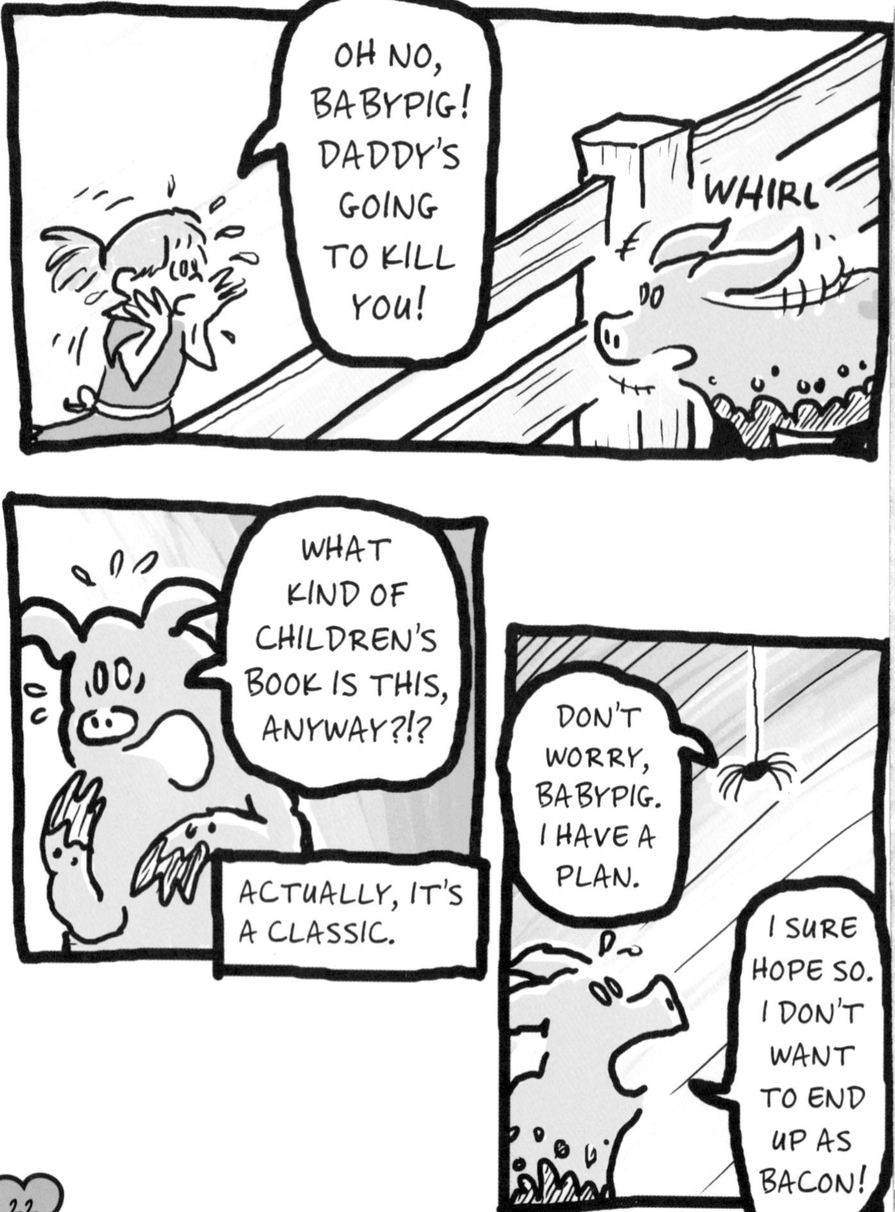
OH NO, BABYPIG! DADDY'S GOING TO KILL YOU!
WHIRL
WHAT KIND OF CHILDREN'S BOOK IS THIS, ANYWAY?!?
ACTUALLY, IT'S A CLASSIC.
DON'T WORRY, BABYPIG. I HAVE A PLAN.
I SURE HOPE SO. I DON'T WANT TO END UP AS BACON!

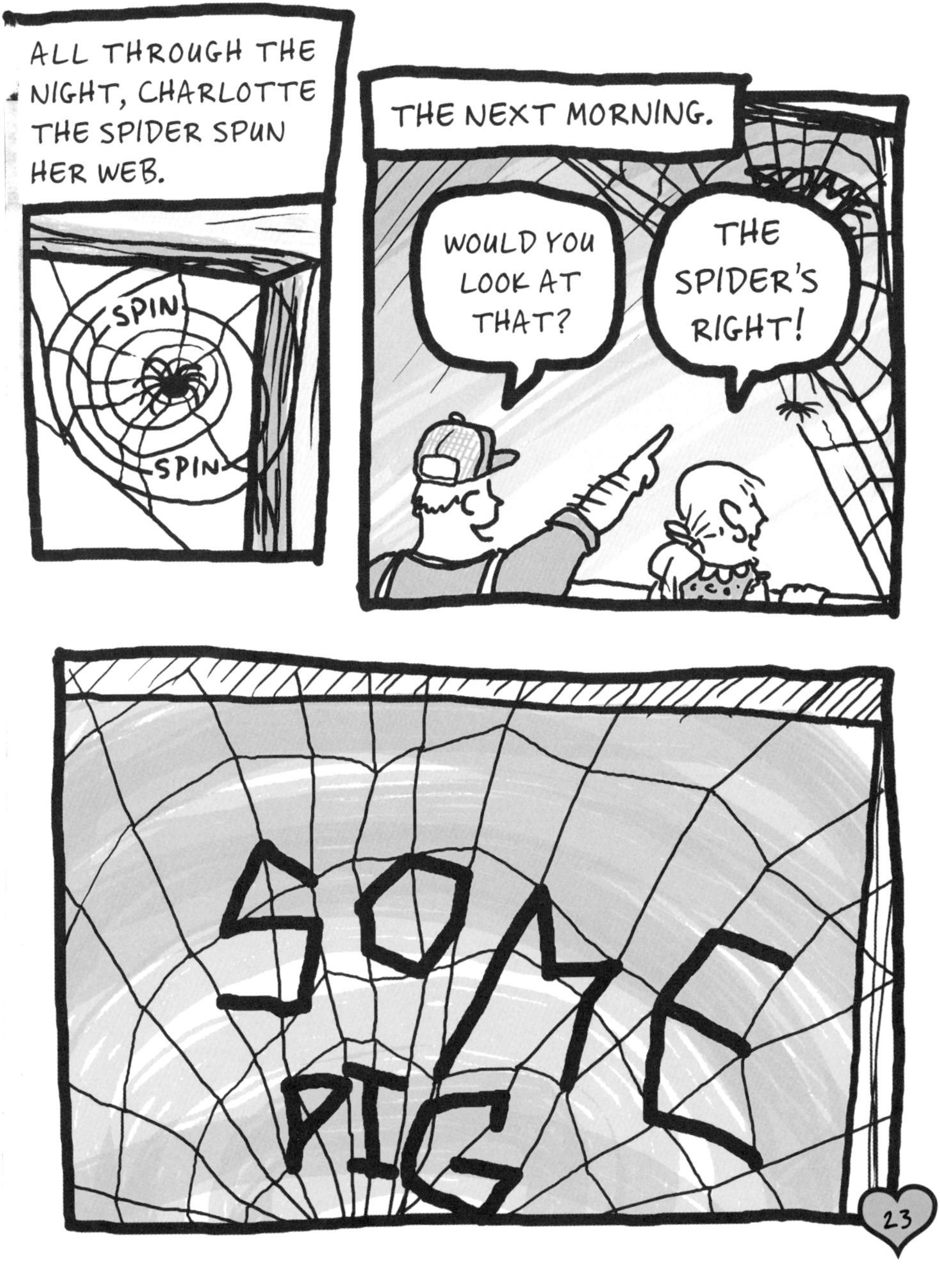
ALL THROUGH THE NIGHT, CHARLOTTE THE SPIDER SPUN HER WEB.
SPIN
SPIN
THE NEXT MORNING.
WOULD YOU LOOK AT THAT?
THE SPIDER'S RIGHT!
SOME PIG

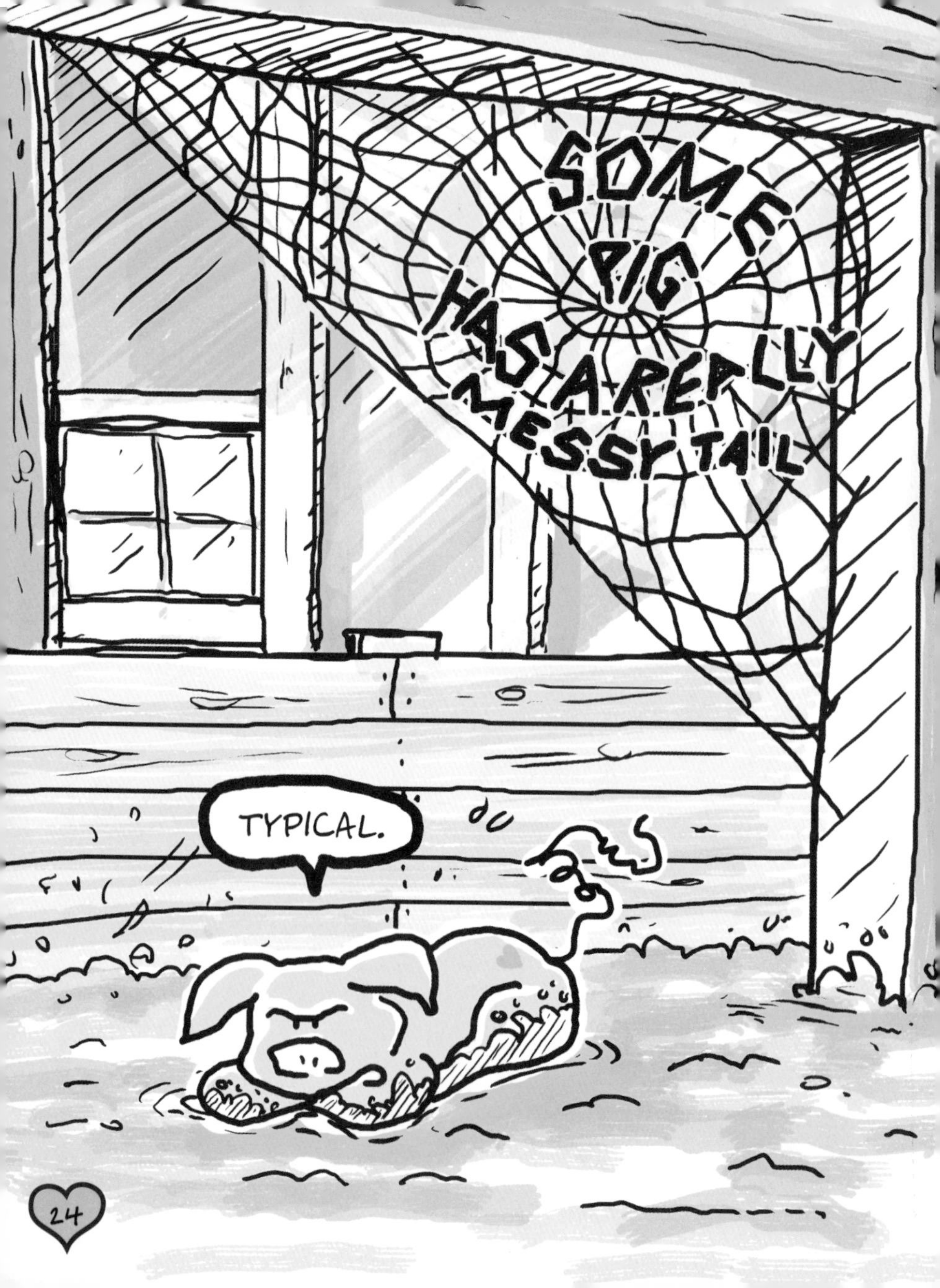
SOME PIG HAS A REALLY MESSY TAIL
TYPICAL.

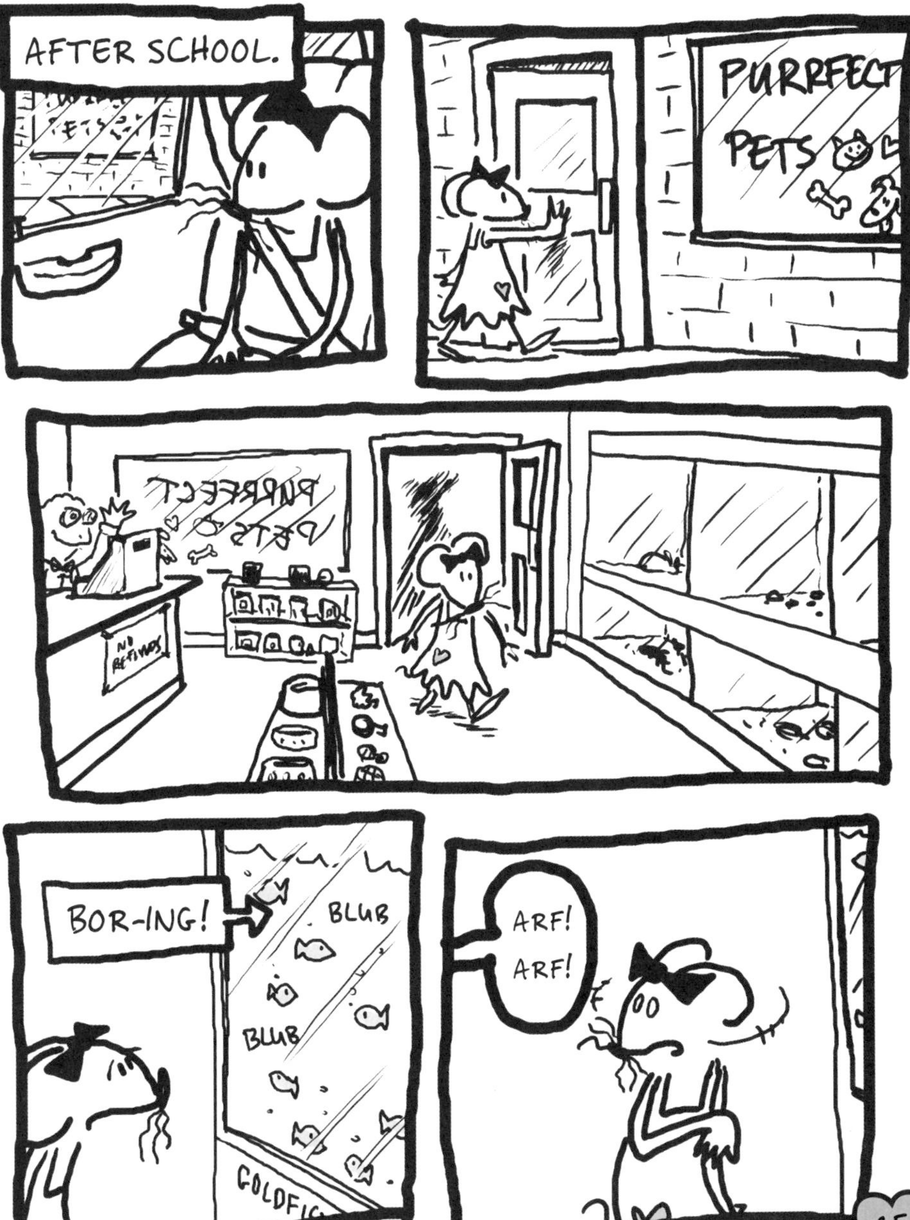
AFTER SCHOOL.
PURRFECT
PETS
NO REFUNDS
BOR-ING!
BLUB
BLUB
ARF!
ARF!

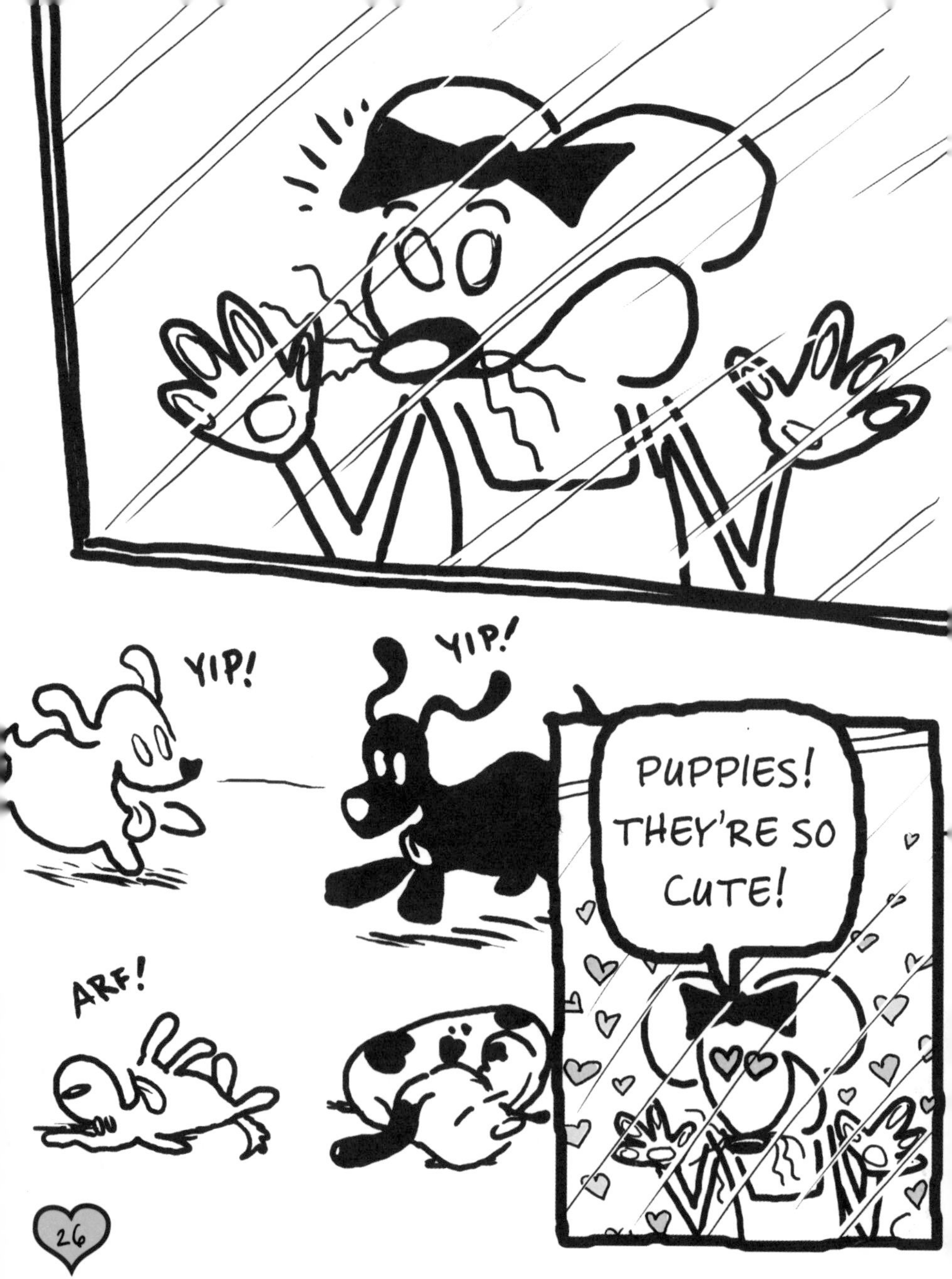
YIP!
YIP!
PUPPIES! THEY'RE SO CUTE!
ARF!

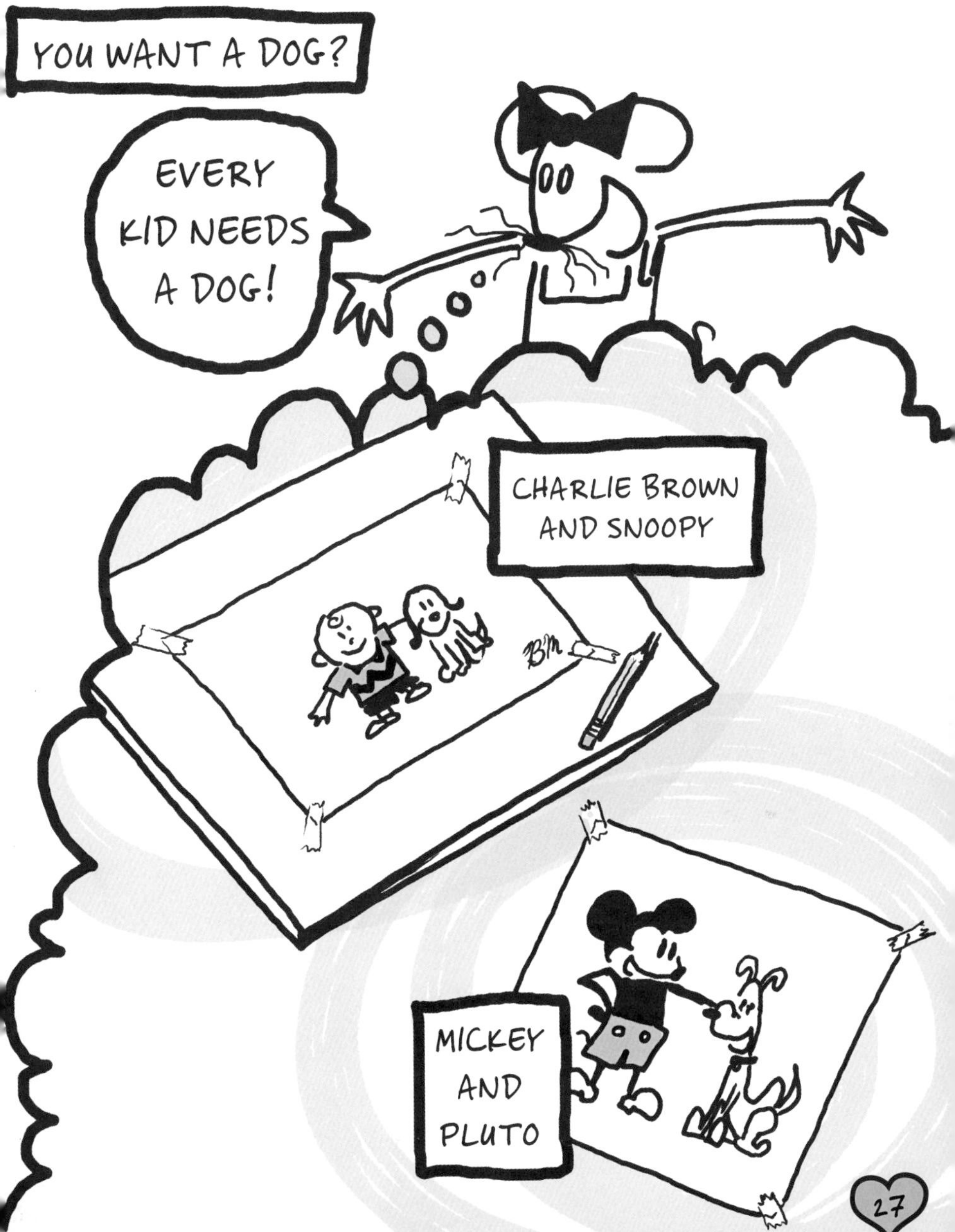
YOU WANT A DOG?
EVERY KID NEEDS A DOG!
CHARLIE BROWN AND SNOOPY
MICKEY AND PLUTO

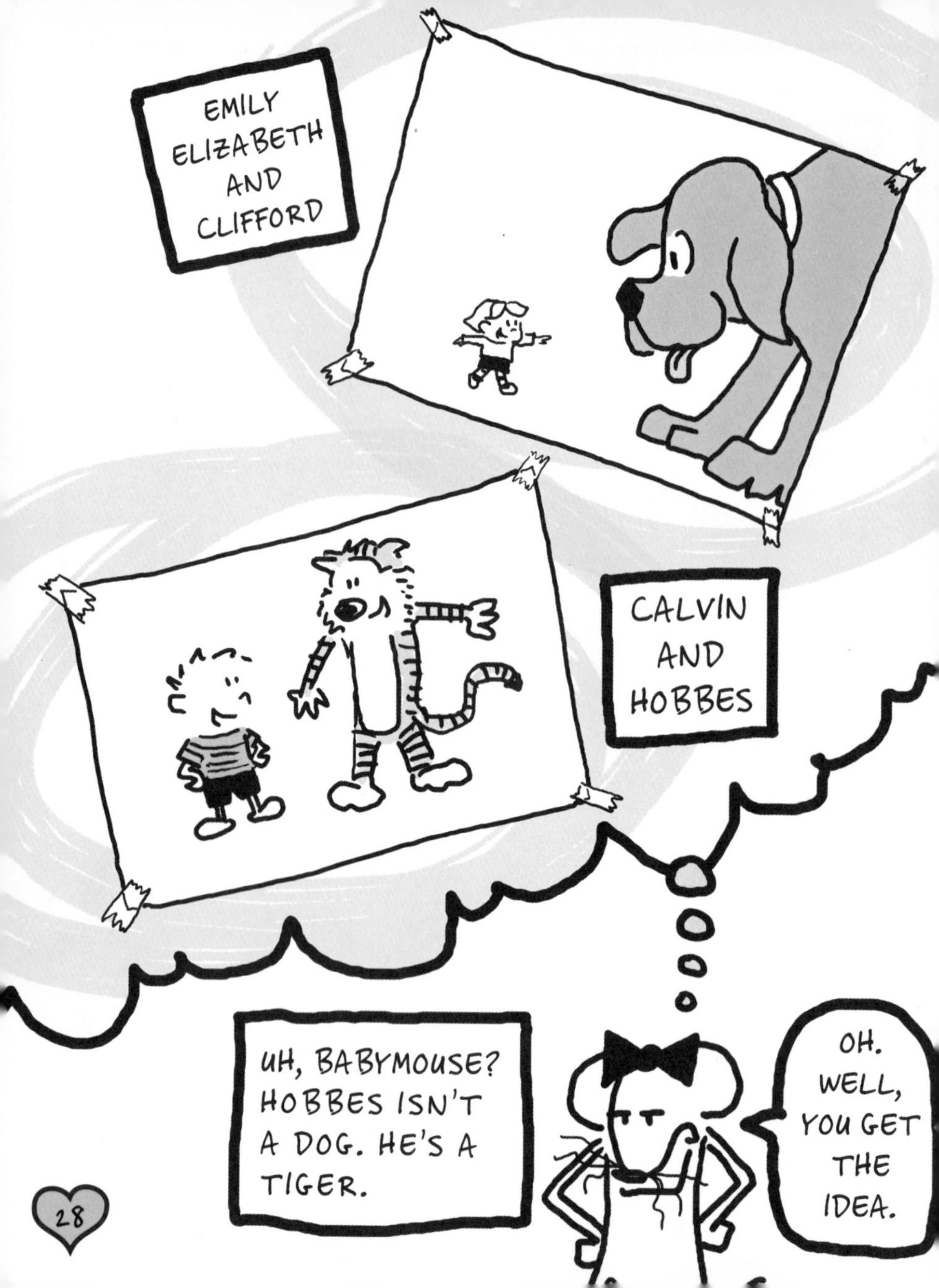
EMILY ELIZABETH AND CLIFFORD
CALVIN AND HOBBES
UH, BABYMOUSE? HOBBES ISN'T A DOG. HE'S A TIGER.
OH. WELL, YOU GET THE IDEA.

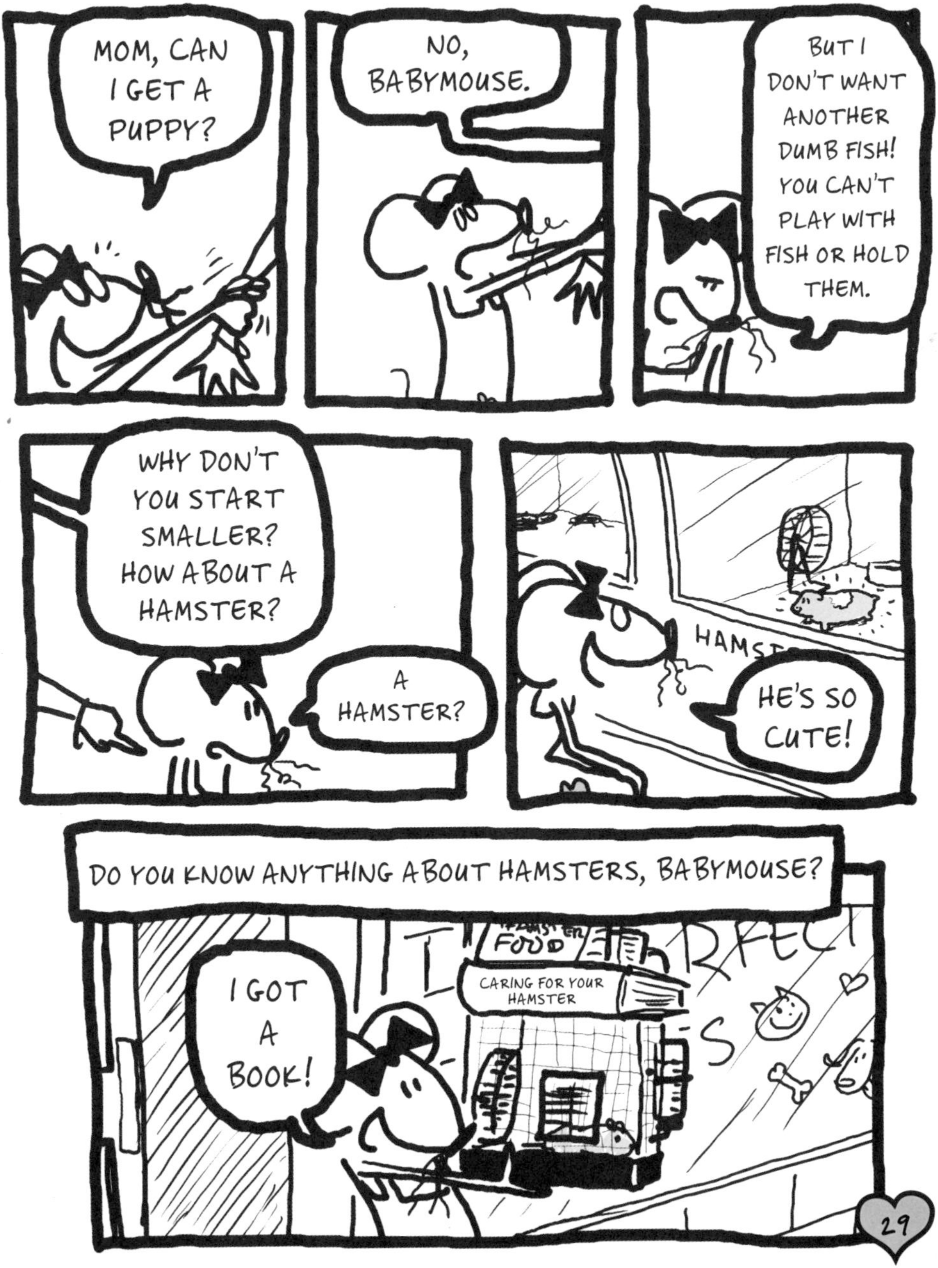
MOM, CAN I GET A PUPPY?
NO, BABYMOUSE.
BUT I DON'T WANT ANOTHER DUMB FISH! YOU CAN'T PLAY WITH FISH OR HOLD THEM.
WHY DON'T YOU START SMALLER? HOW ABOUT A HAMSTER?
A HAMSTER?
HE'S SO CUTE!
DO YOU KNOW ANYTHING ABOUT HAMSTERS, BABYMOUSE?
HAMSTER FOOD
CARING FOR YOUR HAMSTER
I GOT A BOOK!

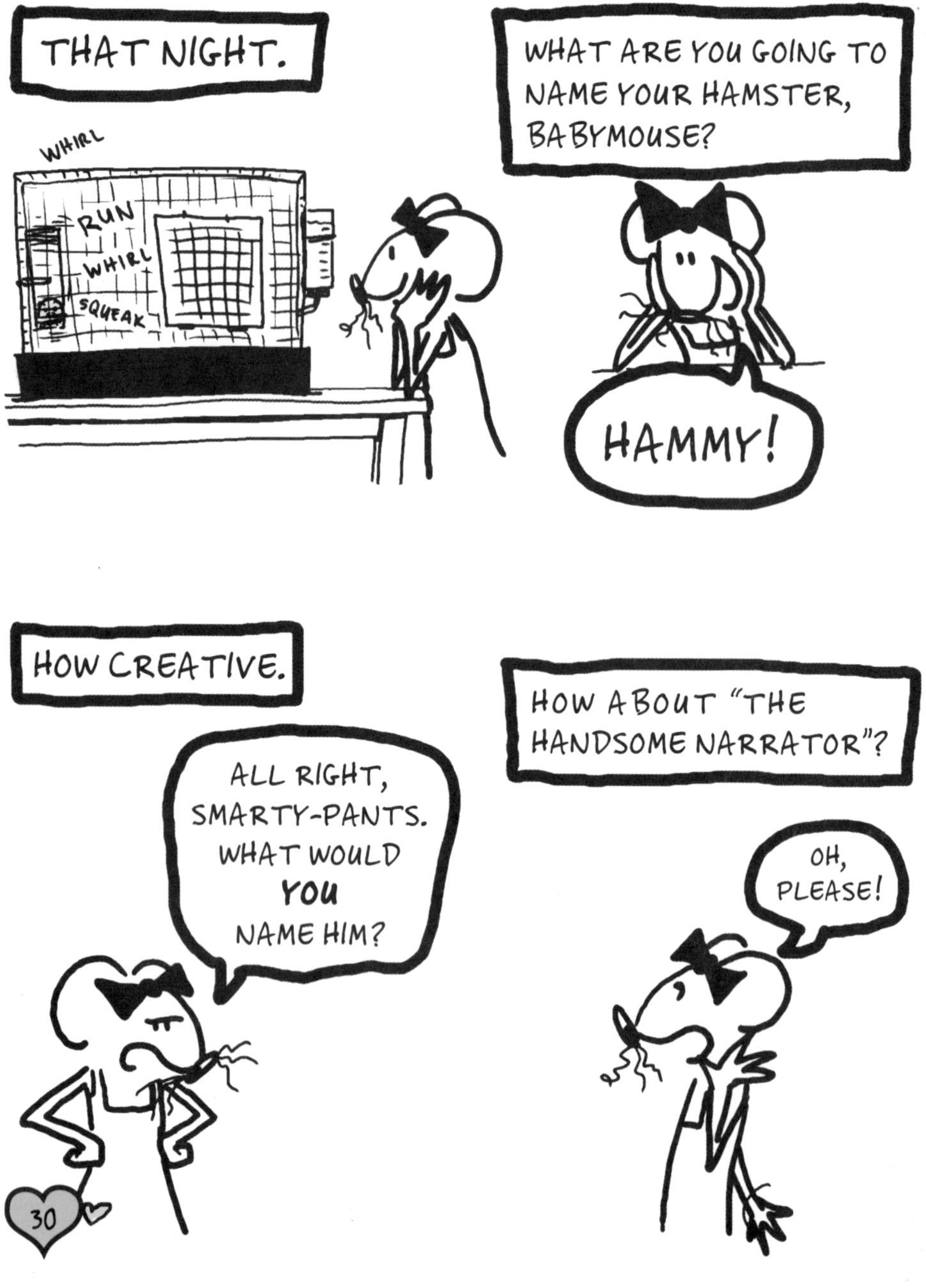
THAT NIGHT.
WHIRL
RUN
WHIRL
SQUEAK
WHAT ARE YOU GOING TO NAME YOUR HAMSTER, BABYMOUSE?
HAMMY!
HOW CREATIVE.
ALL RIGHT, SMARTY-PANTS. WHAT WOULD **YOU** NAME HIM?
HOW ABOUT "THE HANDSOME NARRATOR"?
OH, PLEASE!

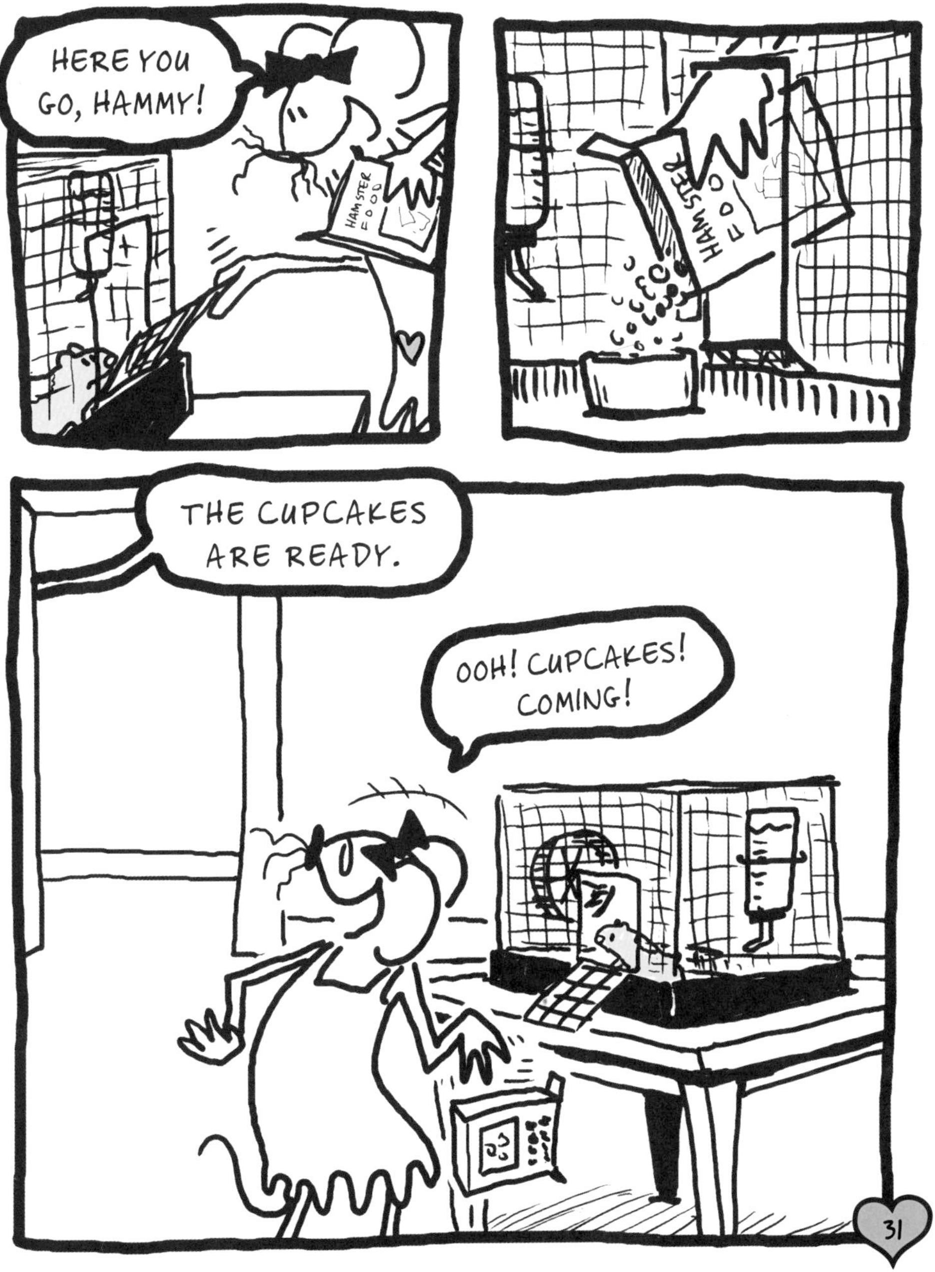
HERE YOU GO, HAMMY!
HAMSTER FOOD
HAMSTER FOOD
THE CUPCAKES ARE READY.
OOH! CUPCAKES! COMING!

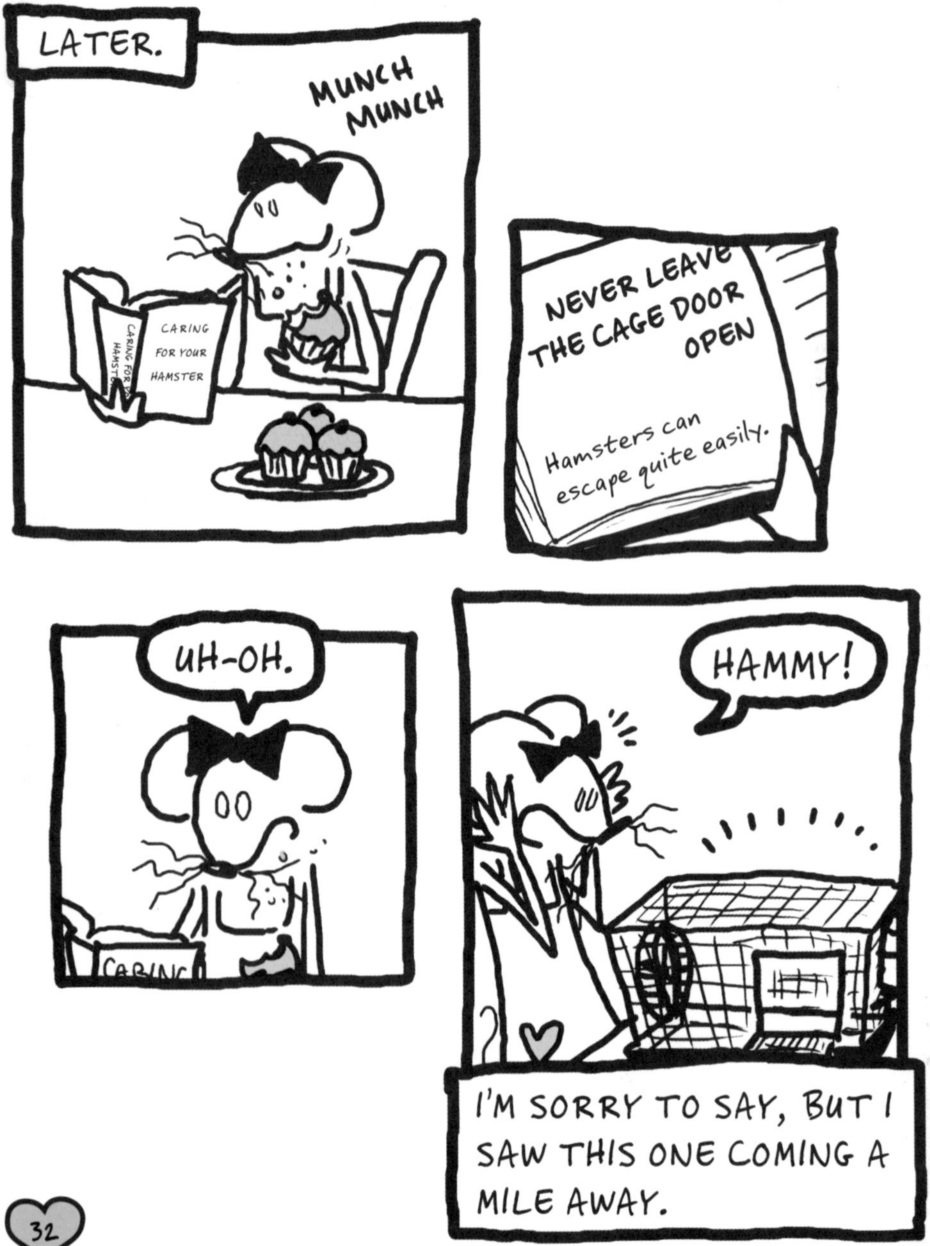
LATER.
MUNCH MUNCH
CARING FOR YOUR HAMSTER
NEVER LEAVE THE CAGE DOOR OPEN
Hamsters can escape quite easily.
UH-OH.
HAMMY!
I'M SORRY TO SAY, BUT I SAW THIS ONE COMING A MILE AWAY.

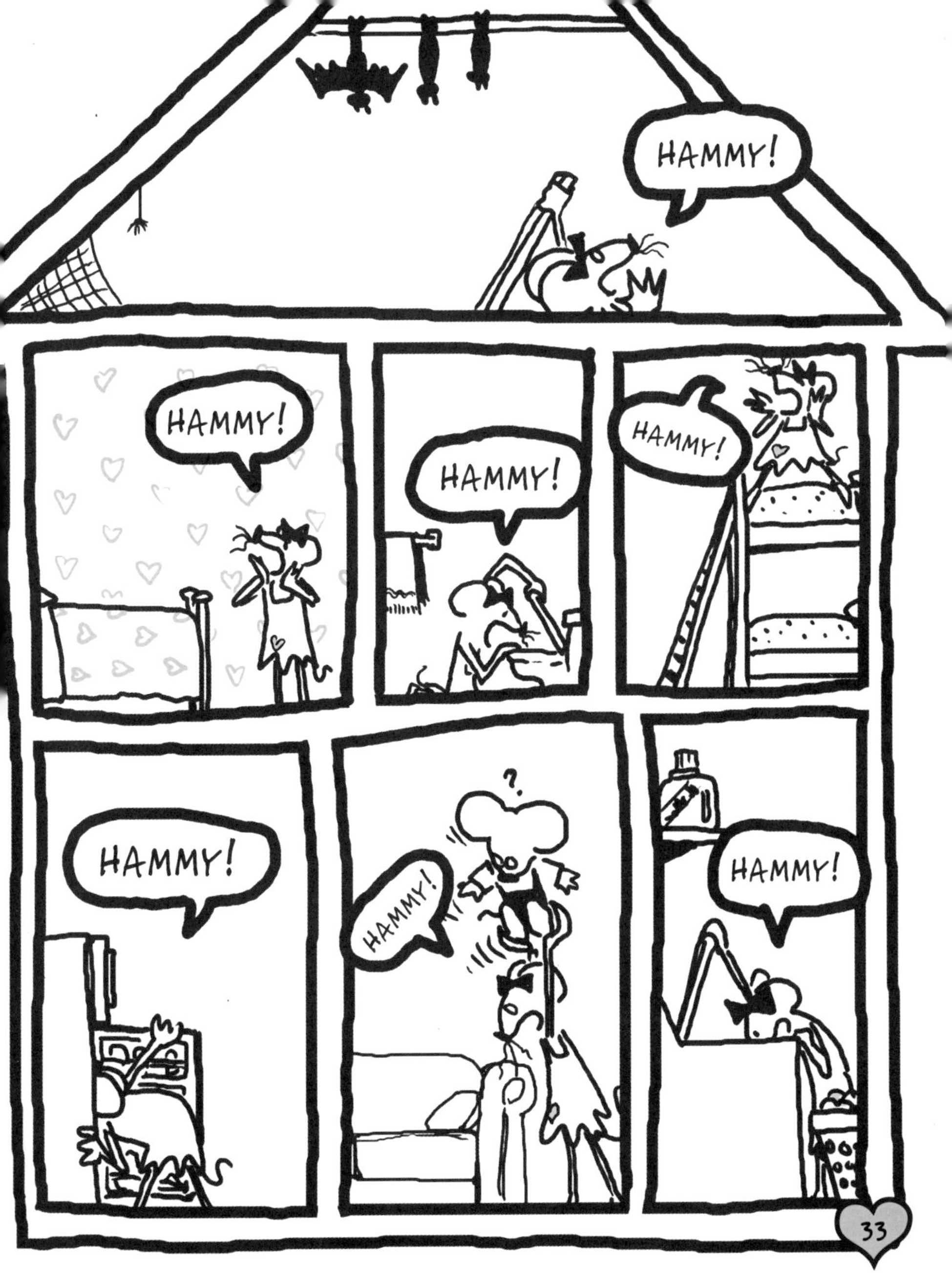
HAMMY!
HAMMY!
HAMMY!
HAMMY!
HAMMY!
HAMMY!
?
HAMMY!

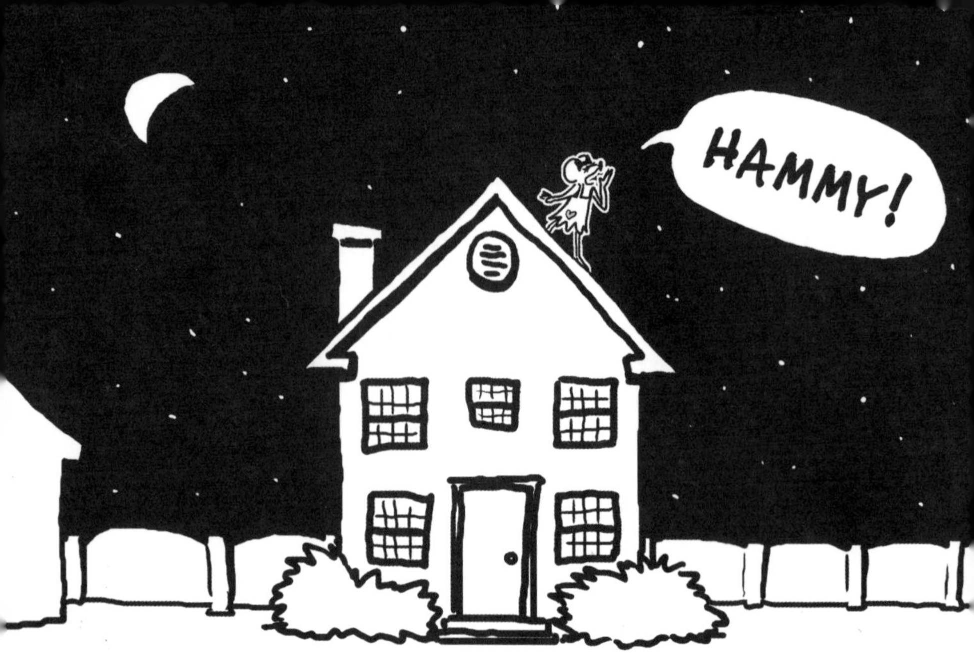
HAMMY!

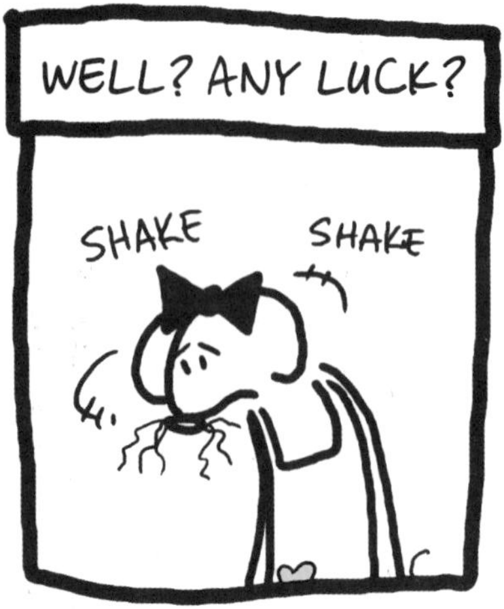
WELL? ANY LUCK?
SHAKE
SHAKE

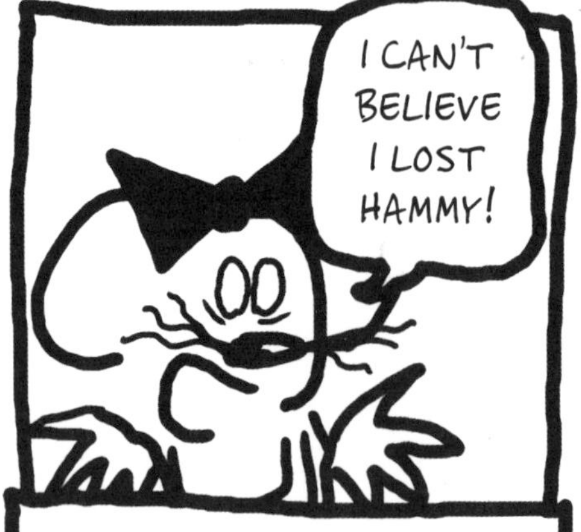
I CAN'T BELIEVE I LOST HAMMY!
ME NEITHER. AND IN ONLY FOUR HOURS. THAT'S A NEW RECORD.

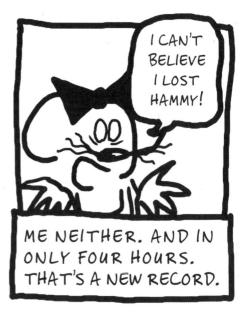

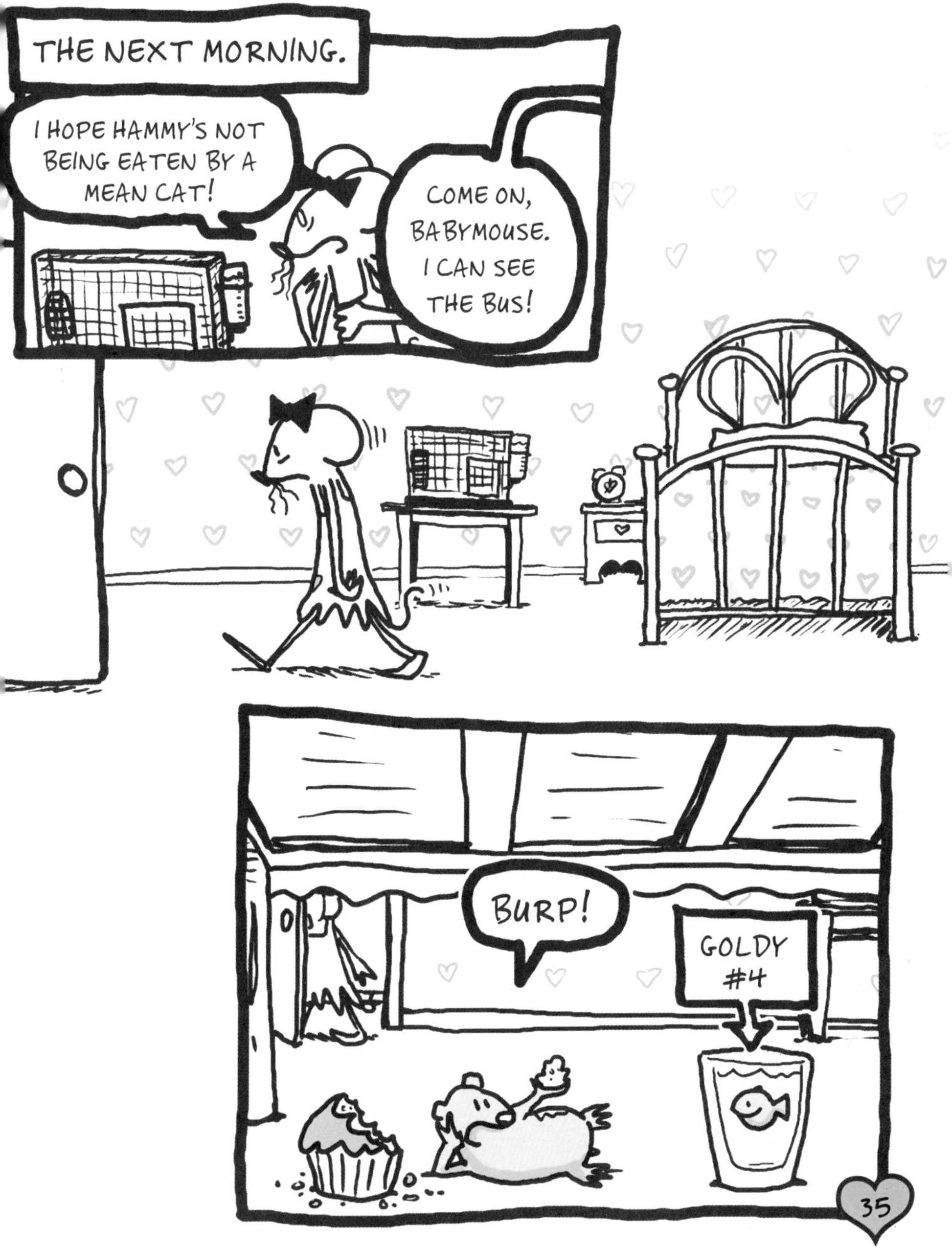
THE NEXT MORNING.
I HOPE HAMMY'S NOT BEING EATEN BY A MEAN CAT!
COME ON, BABYMOUSE. I CAN SEE THE BUS!
BURP!
GOLDY #4

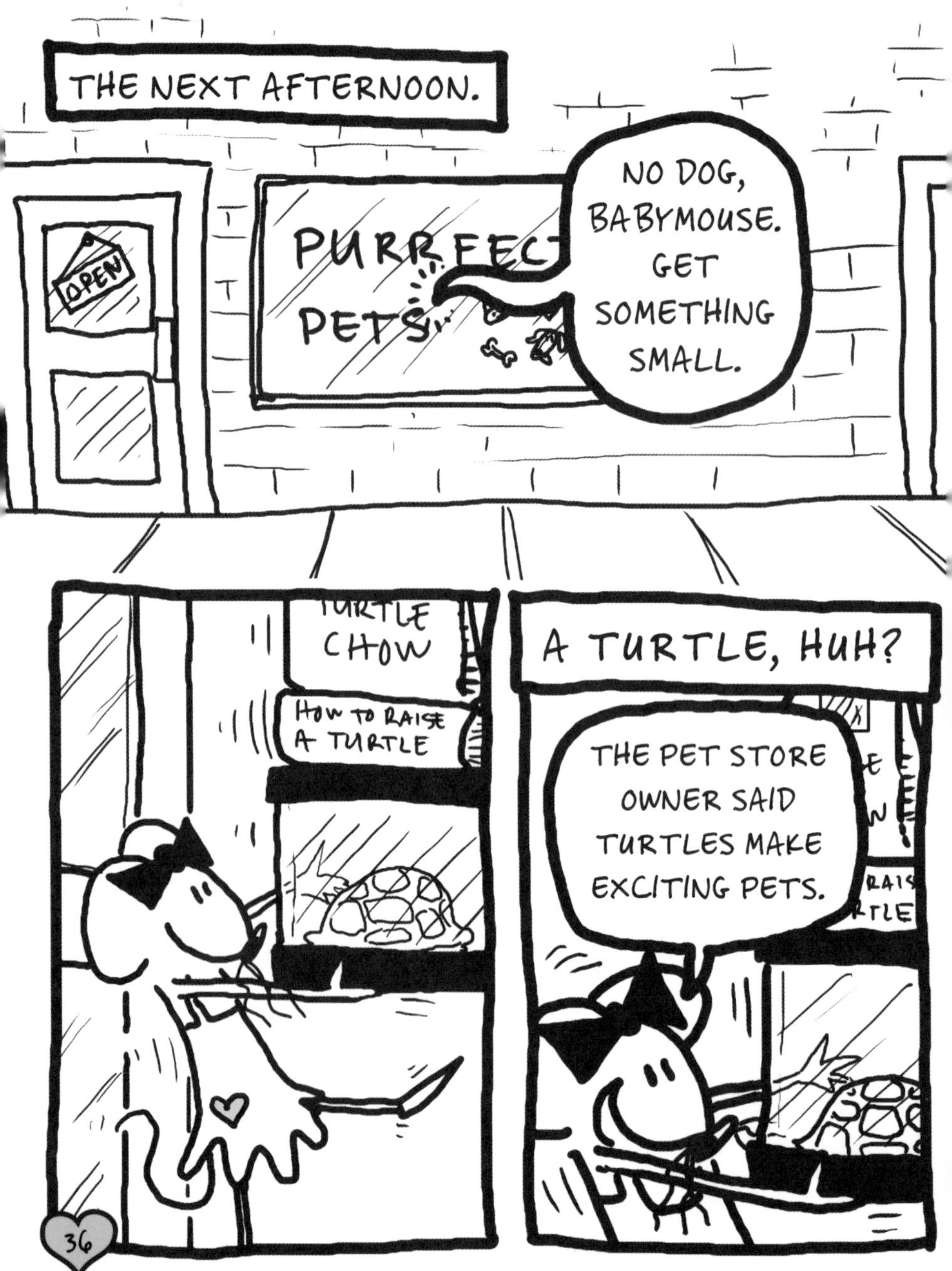
THE NEXT AFTERNOON.
PURRFECT PETS
OPEN
NO DOG, BABYMOUSE. GET SOMETHING SMALL.
TURTLE CHOW
HOW TO RAISE A TURTLE
A TURTLE, HUH?
THE PET STORE OWNER SAID TURTLES MAKE EXCITING PETS.

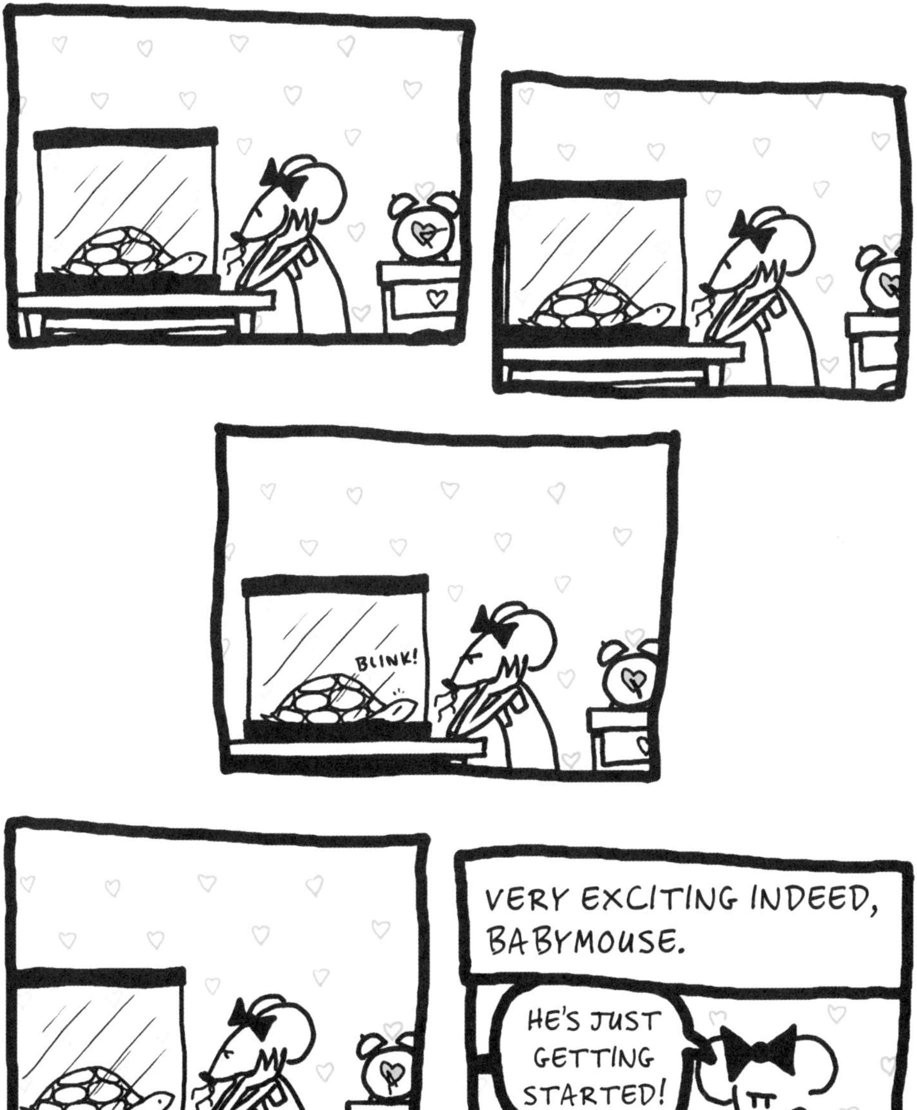
BLINK!
VERY EXCITING INDEED, BABYMOUSE.
HE'S JUST GETTING STARTED!

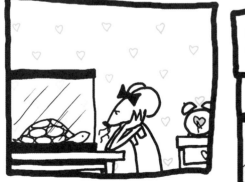

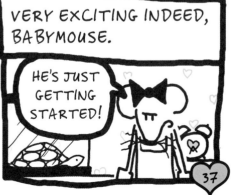

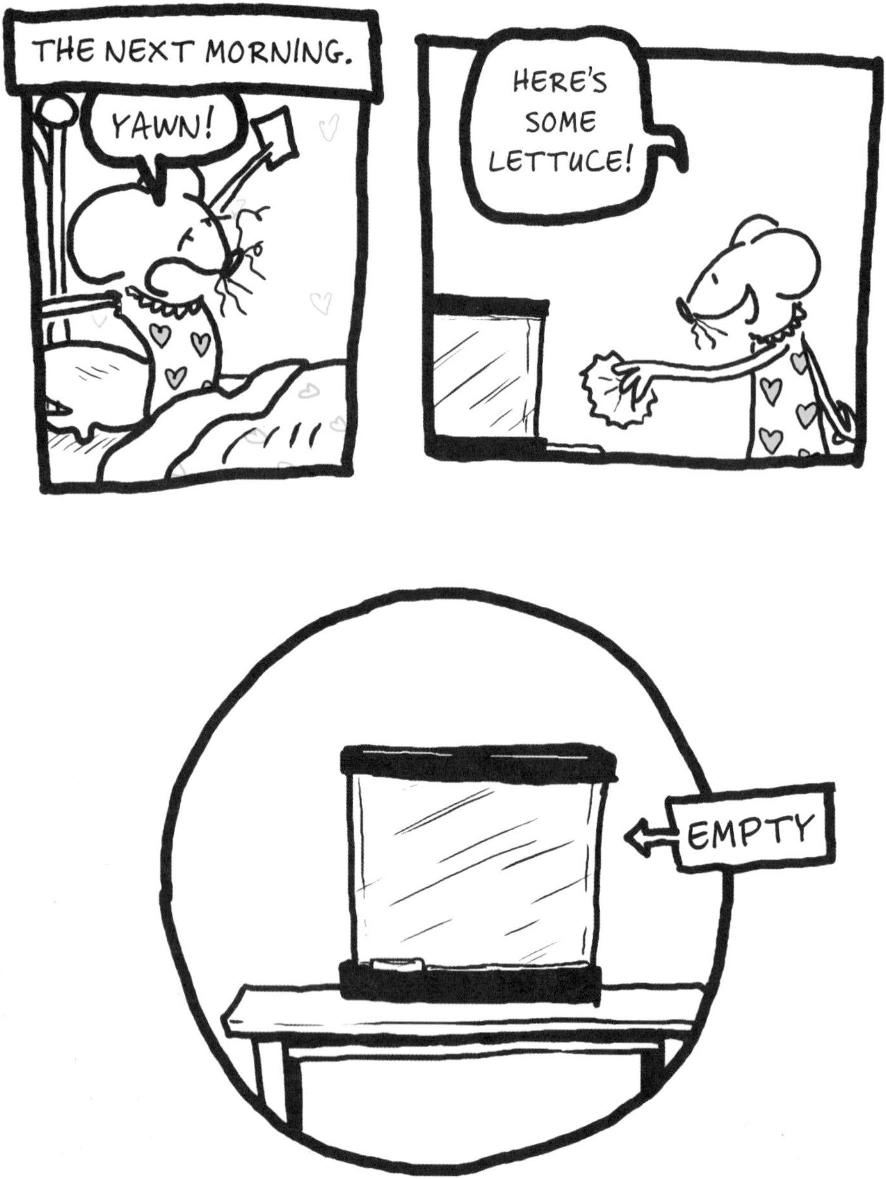
THE NEXT MORNING.
YAWN!
HERE'S SOME LETTUCE!
EMPTY

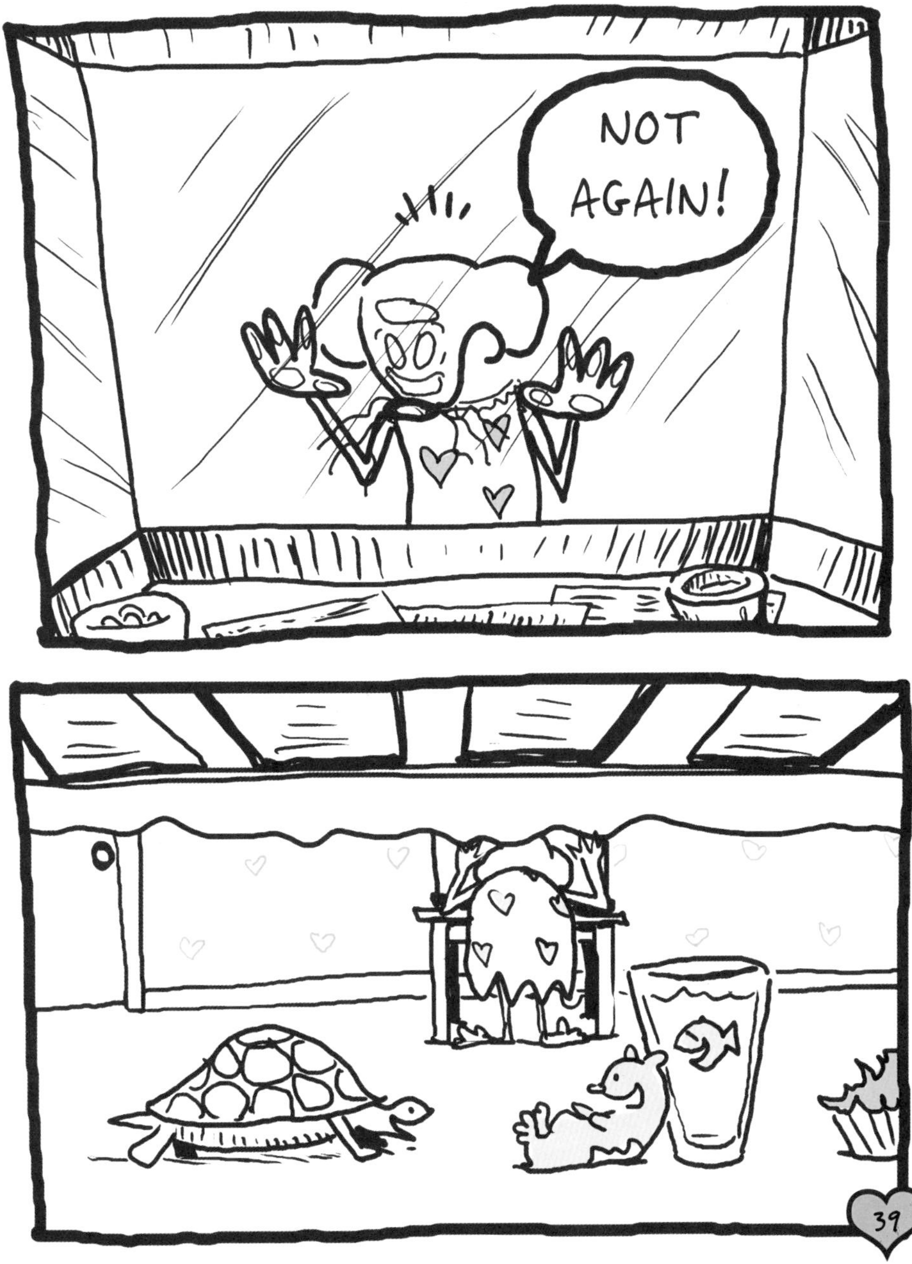
NOT AGAIN!

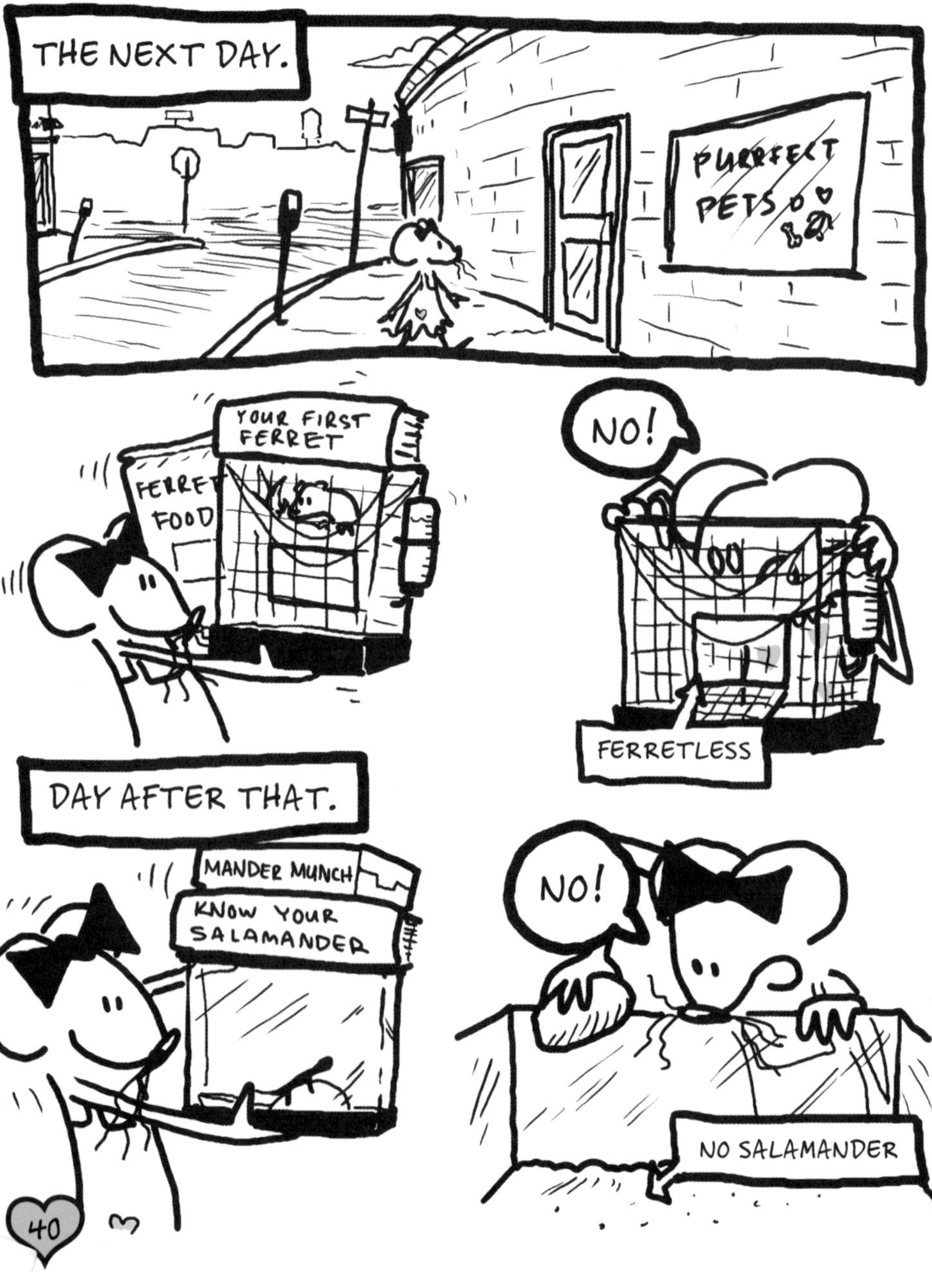
THE NEXT DAY.
PURRFECT PETS
YOUR FIRST FERRET
FERRET FOOD
NO!
FERRETLESS
DAY AFTER THAT.
MANDER MUNCH
KNOW YOUR SALAMANDER
NO!
NO SALAMANDER

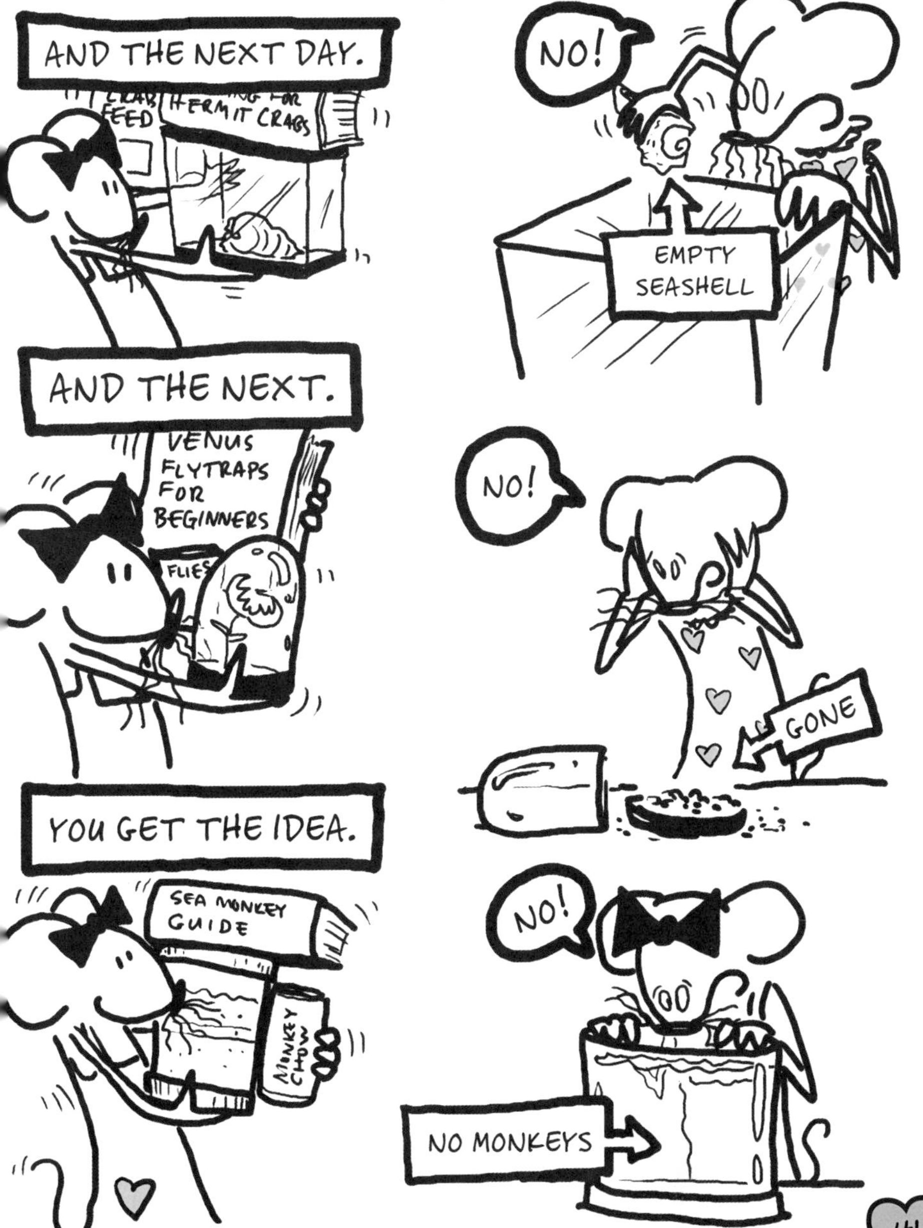
AND THE NEXT DAY.
CRAB FEED
HERMIT CRABS
NO!
EMPTY SEASHELL
AND THE NEXT.
VENUS FLYTRAPS FOR BEGINNERS
FLIES
NO!
GONE
YOU GET THE IDEA.
SEA MONKEY GUIDE
MONKEY CHOW
NO!
NO MONKEYS

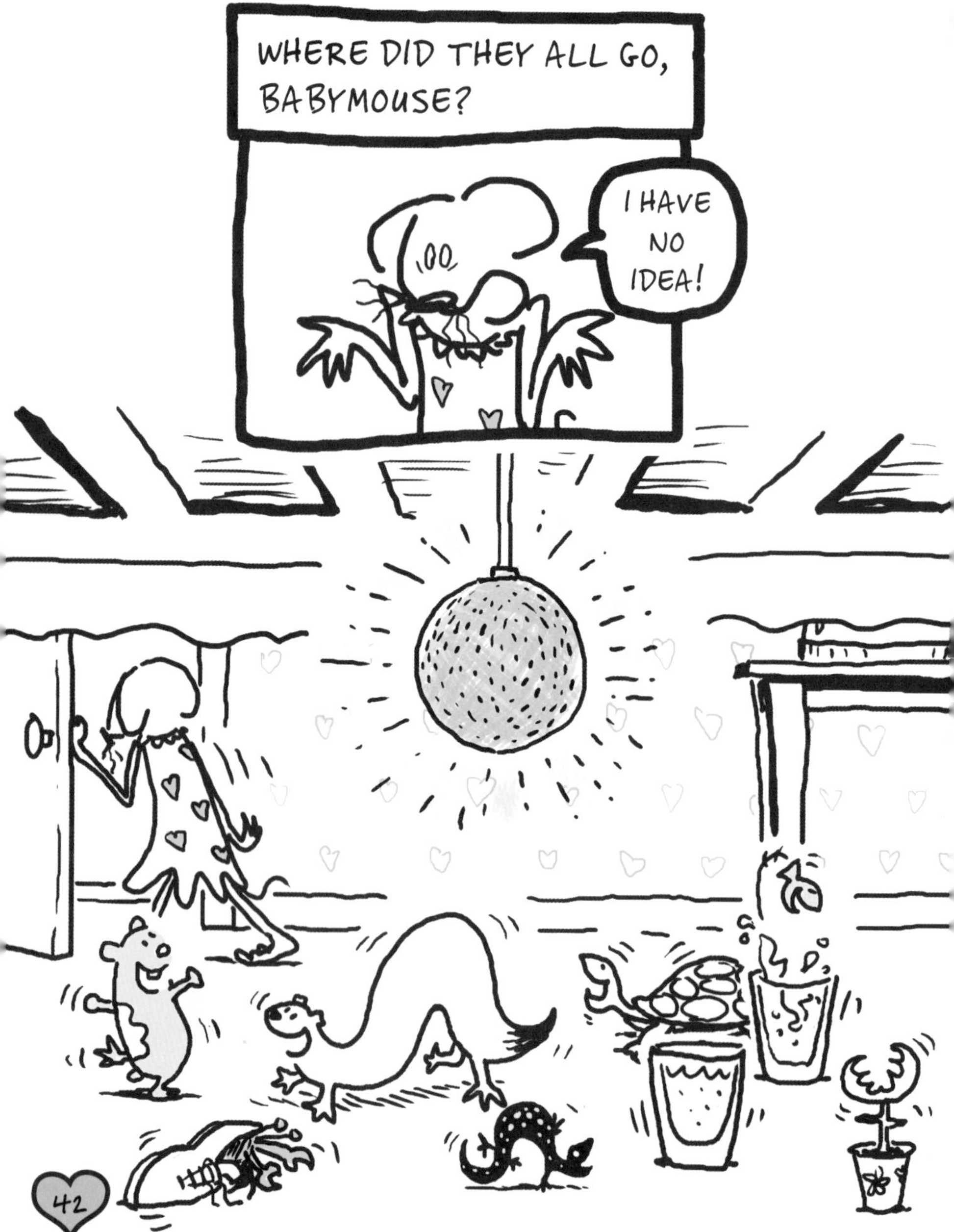
WHERE DID THEY ALL GO, BABYMOUSE?
I HAVE NO IDEA!

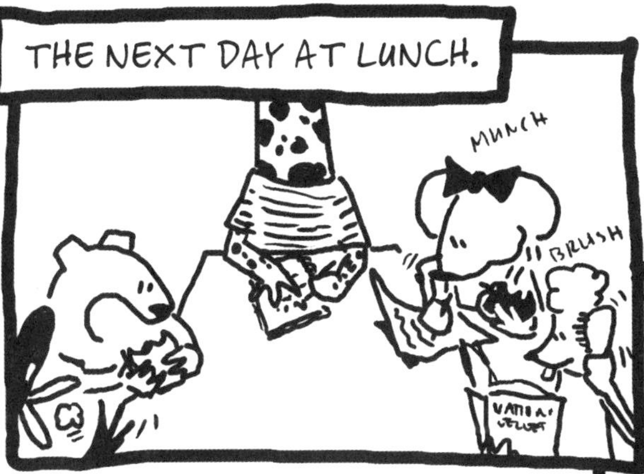
THE NEXT DAY AT LUNCH.
MUNCH
BRUSH

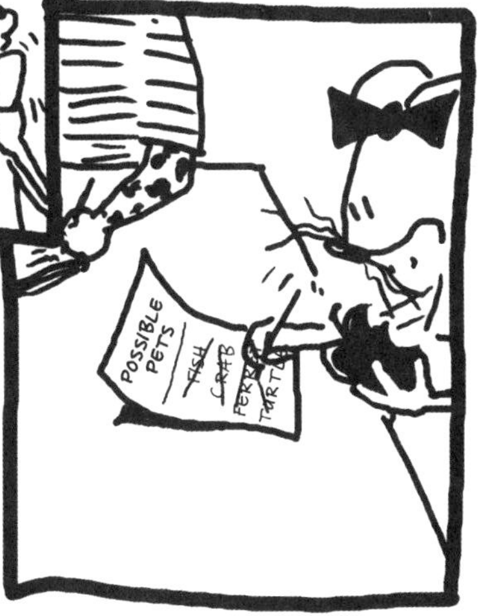
POSSIBLE PETS
FISH
CRAB

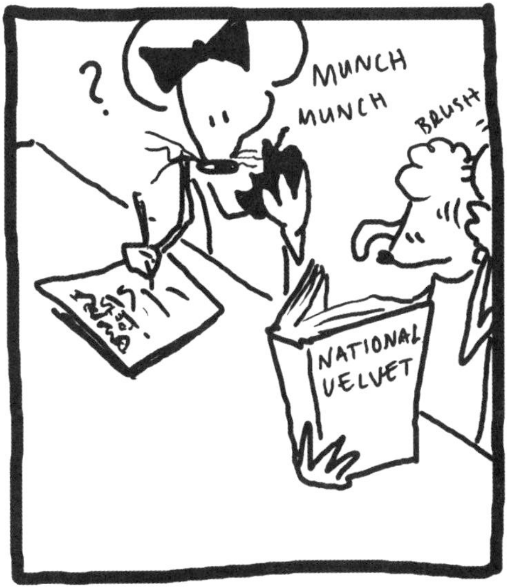
?
MUNCH
MUNCH
BRUSH
NATIONAL VELVET

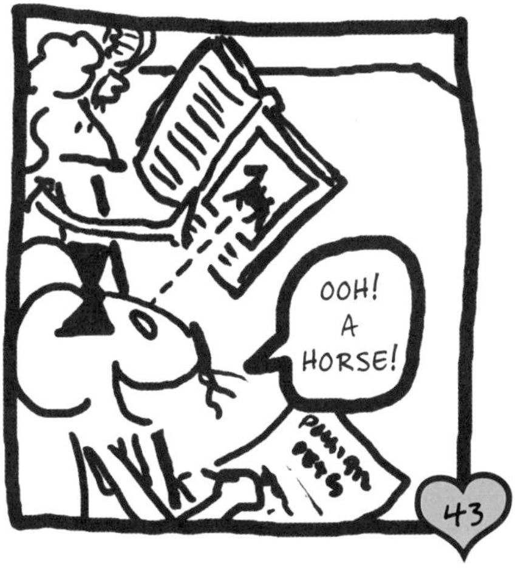
OOH! A HORSE!

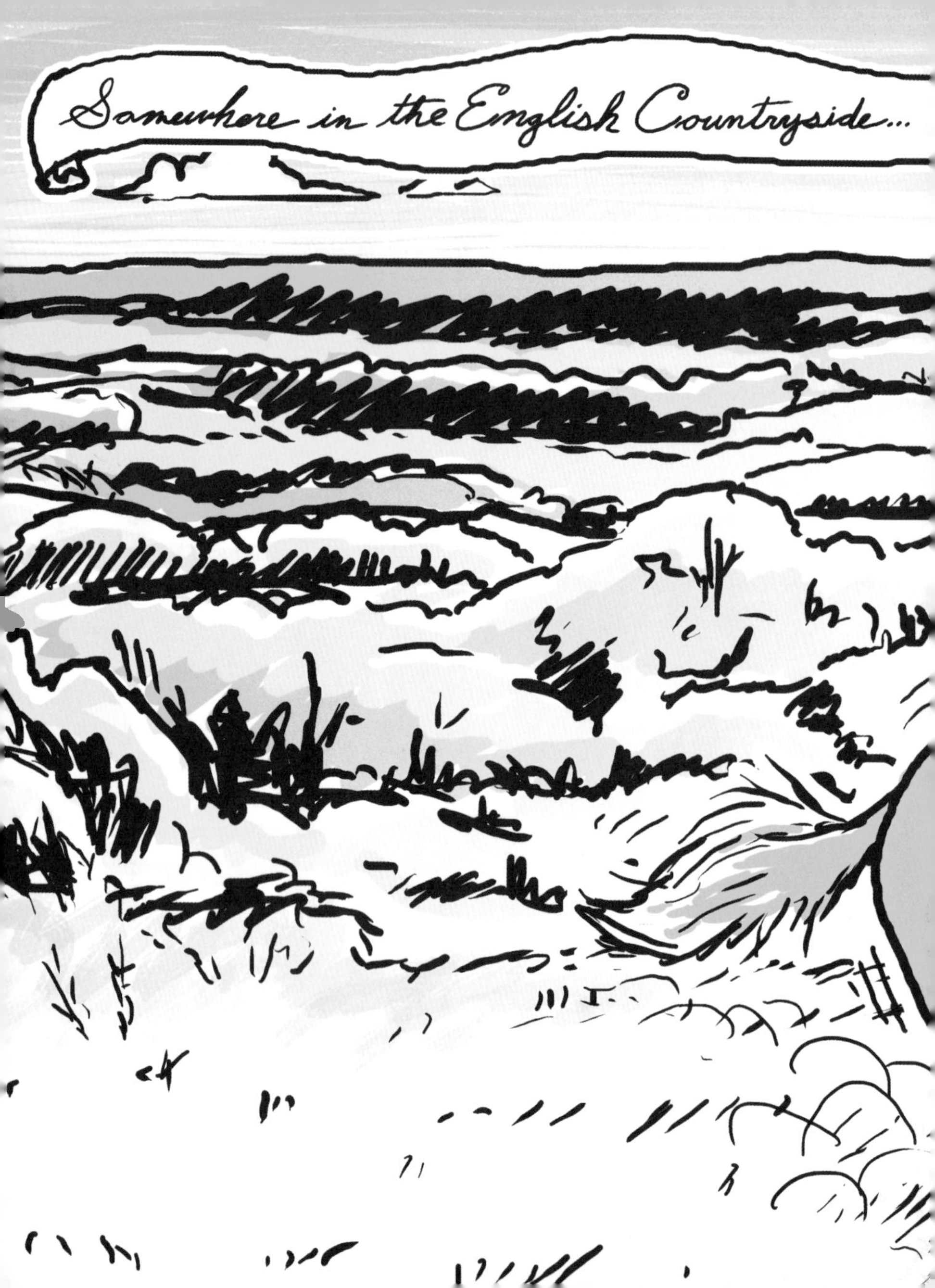
Somewhere in the English Countryside...

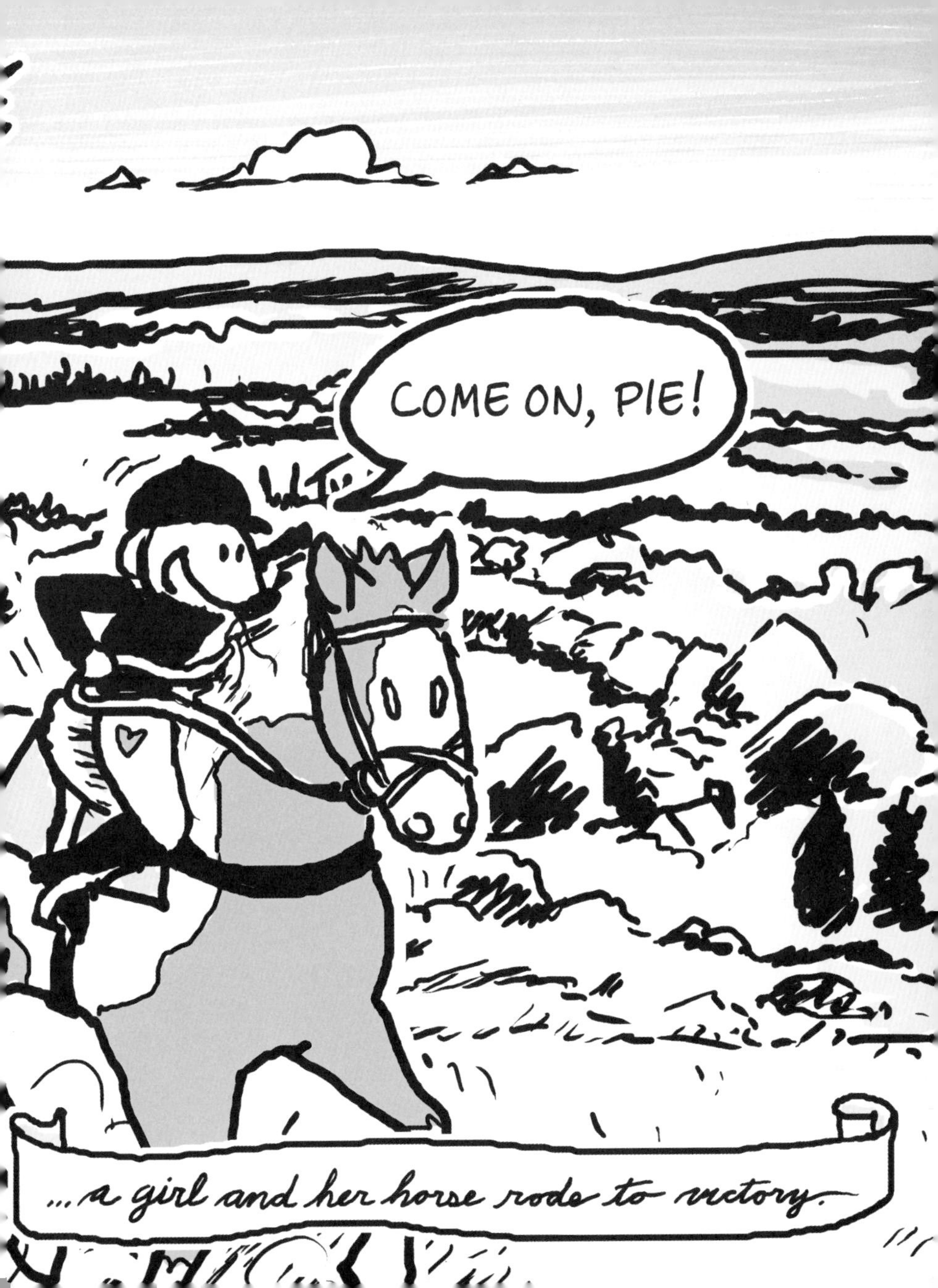
COME ON, PIE!
...a girl and her horse rode to victory.

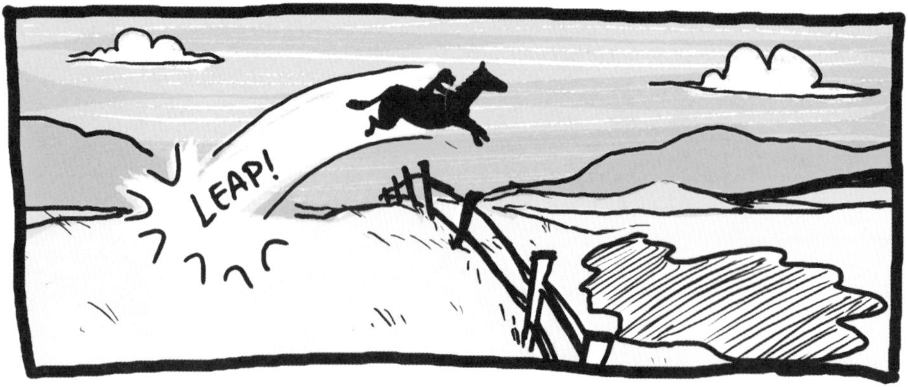
LEAP!

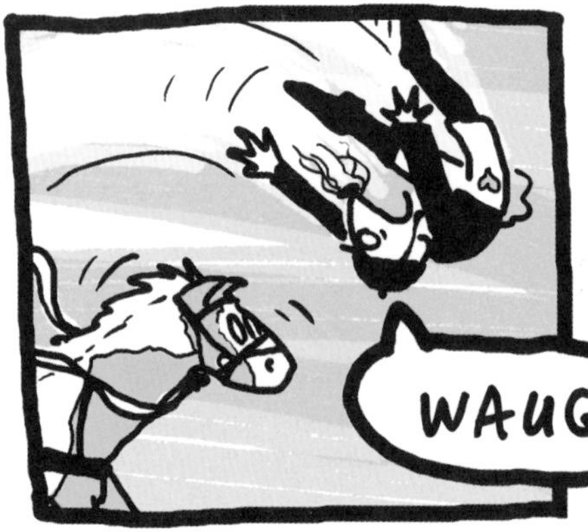
WAUGH!

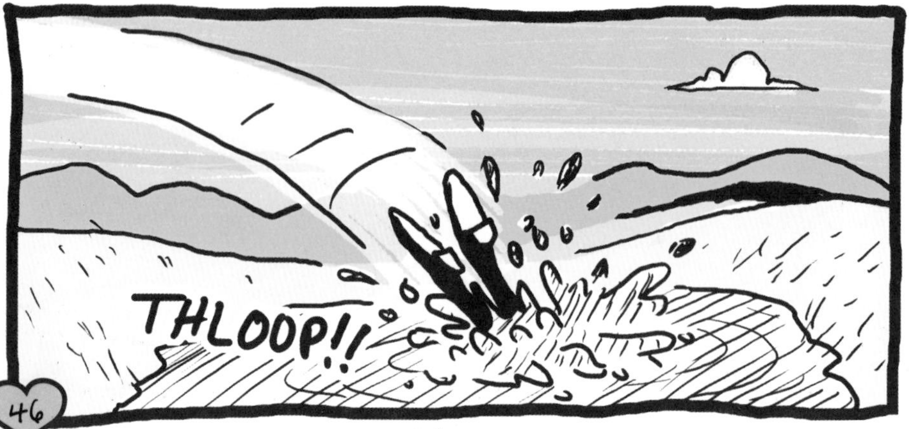
THLOOP!!

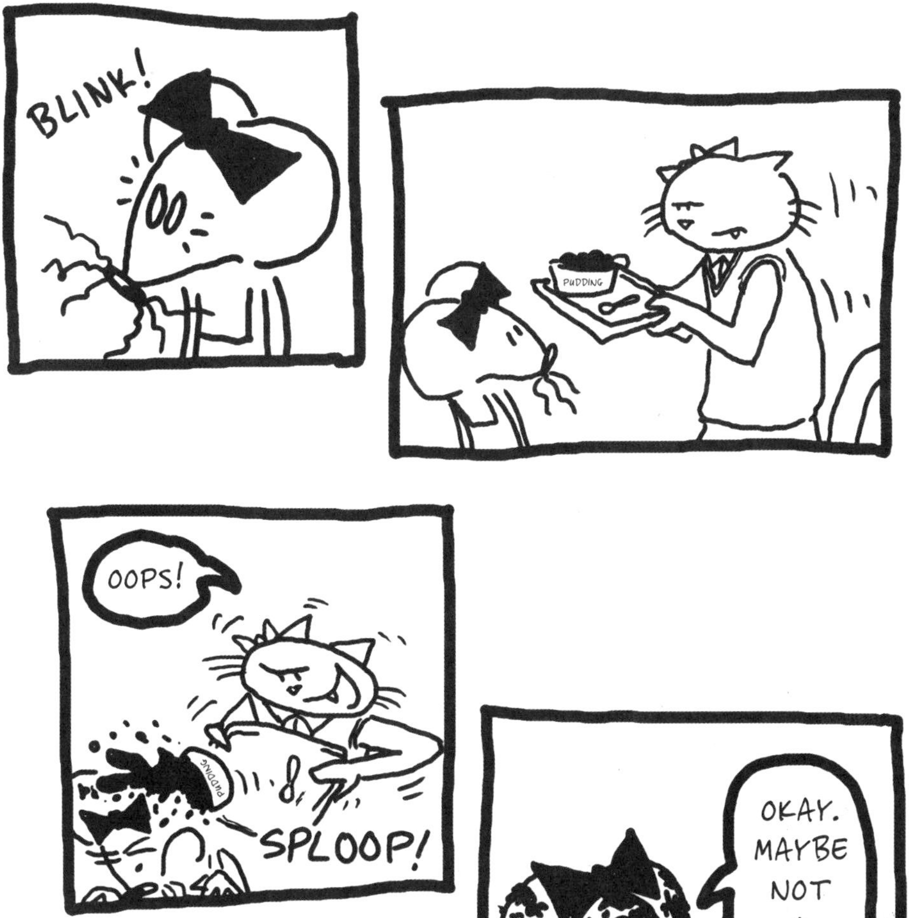
BLINK!
PUDDING
OOPS!
PUDDING
SPLOOP!
OKAY. MAYBE NOT A HORSE.
PUDDING

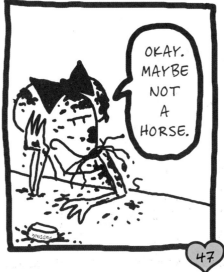

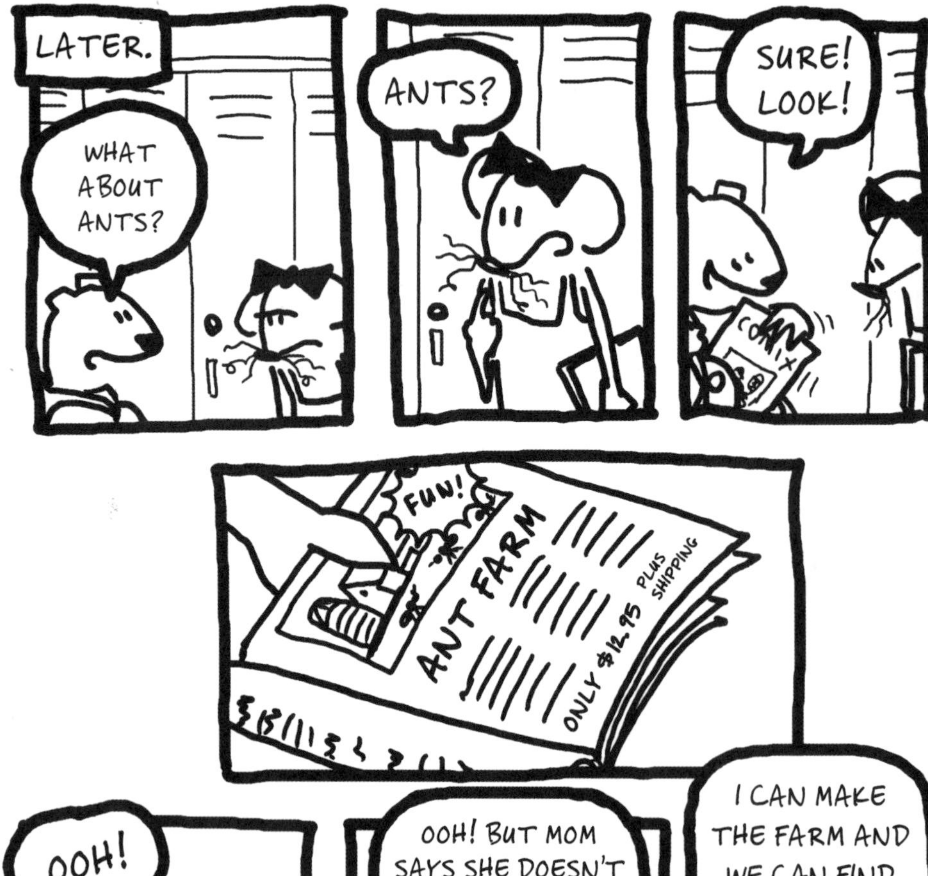
LATER.
WHAT ABOUT ANTS?
ANTS?
SURE! LOOK!
FUN!
ANT FARM
ONLY $12.95 PLUS SHIPPING
OOH!
OOH! BUT MOM SAYS SHE DOESN'T WANT TO SPEND ANY MORE MONEY ON PETS WHEN I KEEP LOSING THEM.
I CAN MAKE THE FARM AND WE CAN FIND THE ANTS OURSELVES FOR FREE!
WOW! THANKS, WILSON!

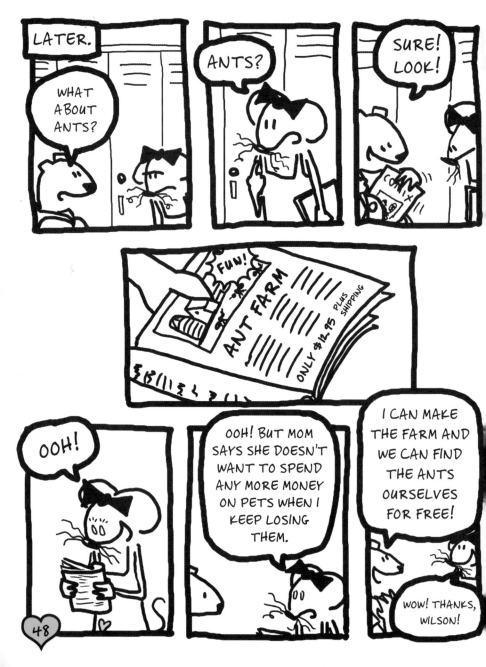

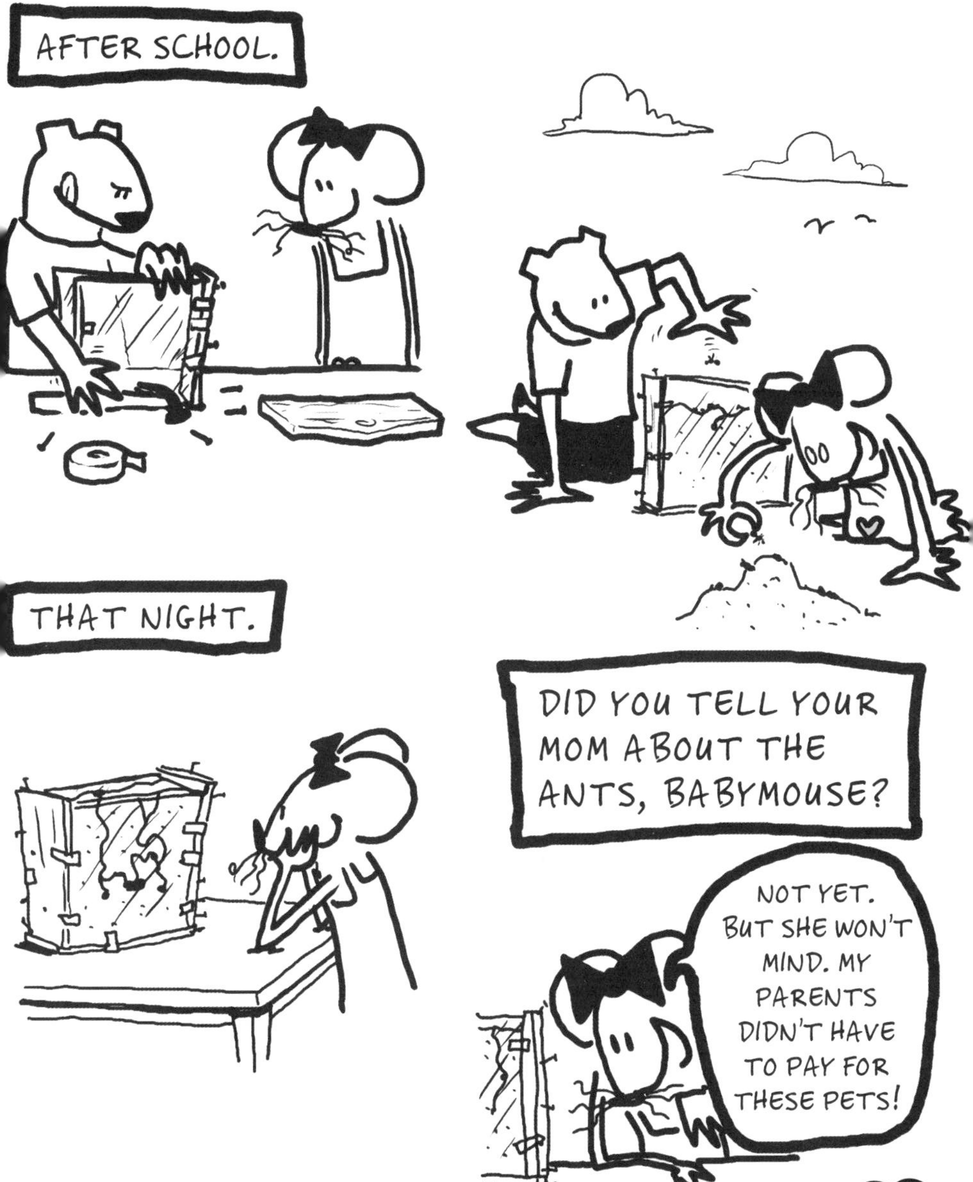
AFTER SCHOOL.
THAT NIGHT.
DID YOU TELL YOUR MOM ABOUT THE ANTS, BABYMOUSE?
NOT YET. BUT SHE WON'T MIND. MY PARENTS DIDN'T HAVE TO PAY FOR THESE PETS!

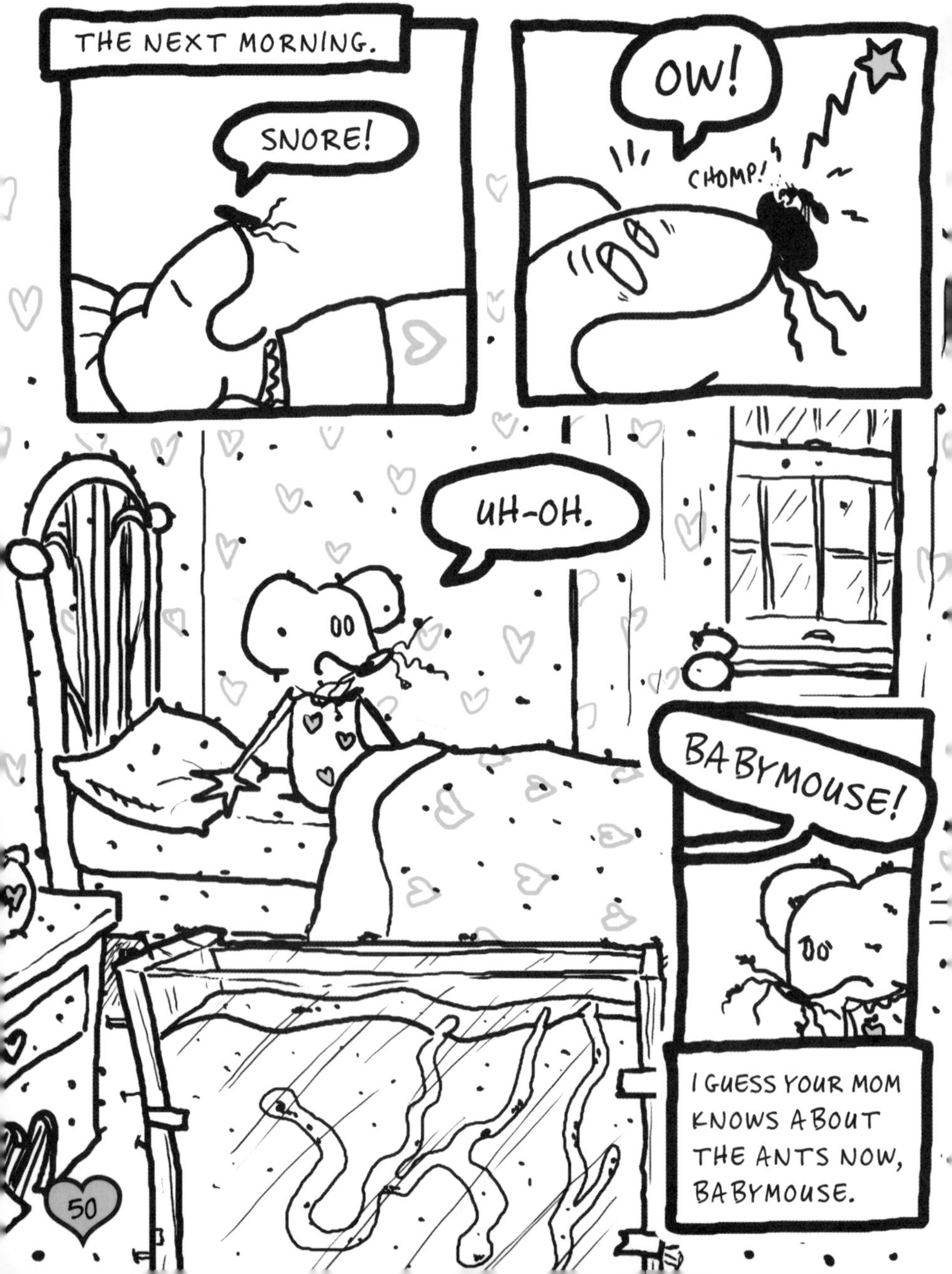
THE NEXT MORNING.
SNORE!
OW!
CHOMP!
UH-OH.
BABYMOUSE!
I GUESS YOUR MOM KNOWS ABOUT THE ANTS NOW, BABYMOUSE.

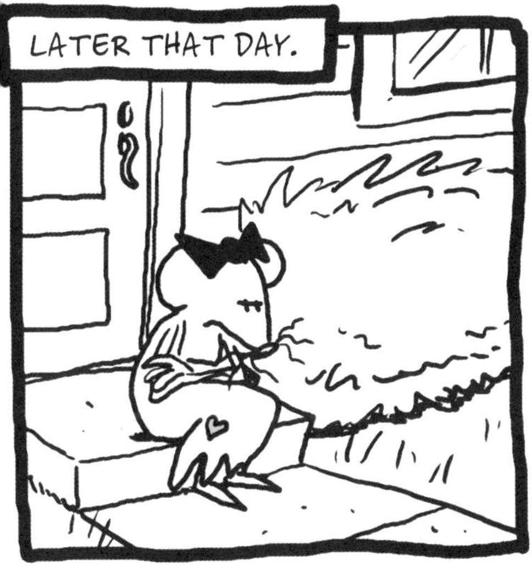
LATER THAT DAY.

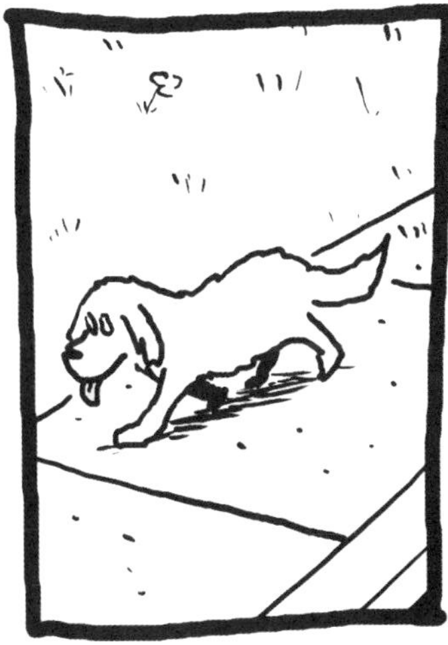

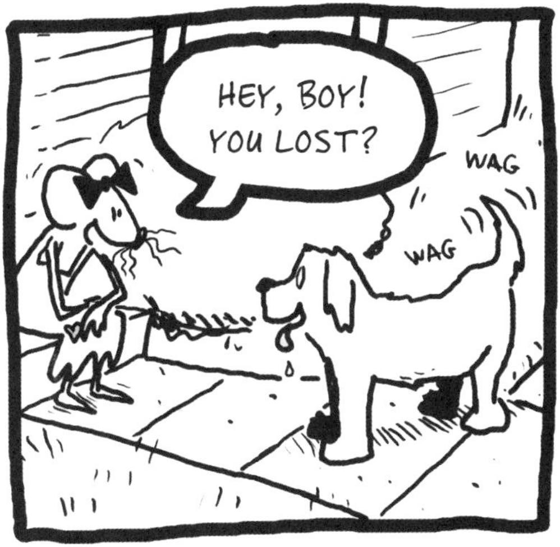
HEY, BOY!
YOU LOST?
WAG
WAG

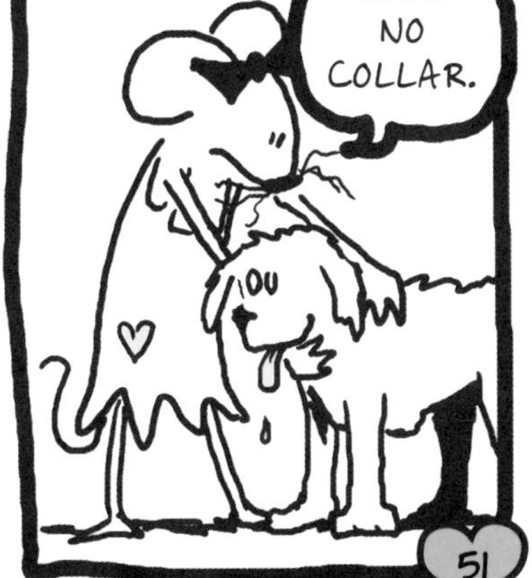
HMM.
NO
COLLAR.

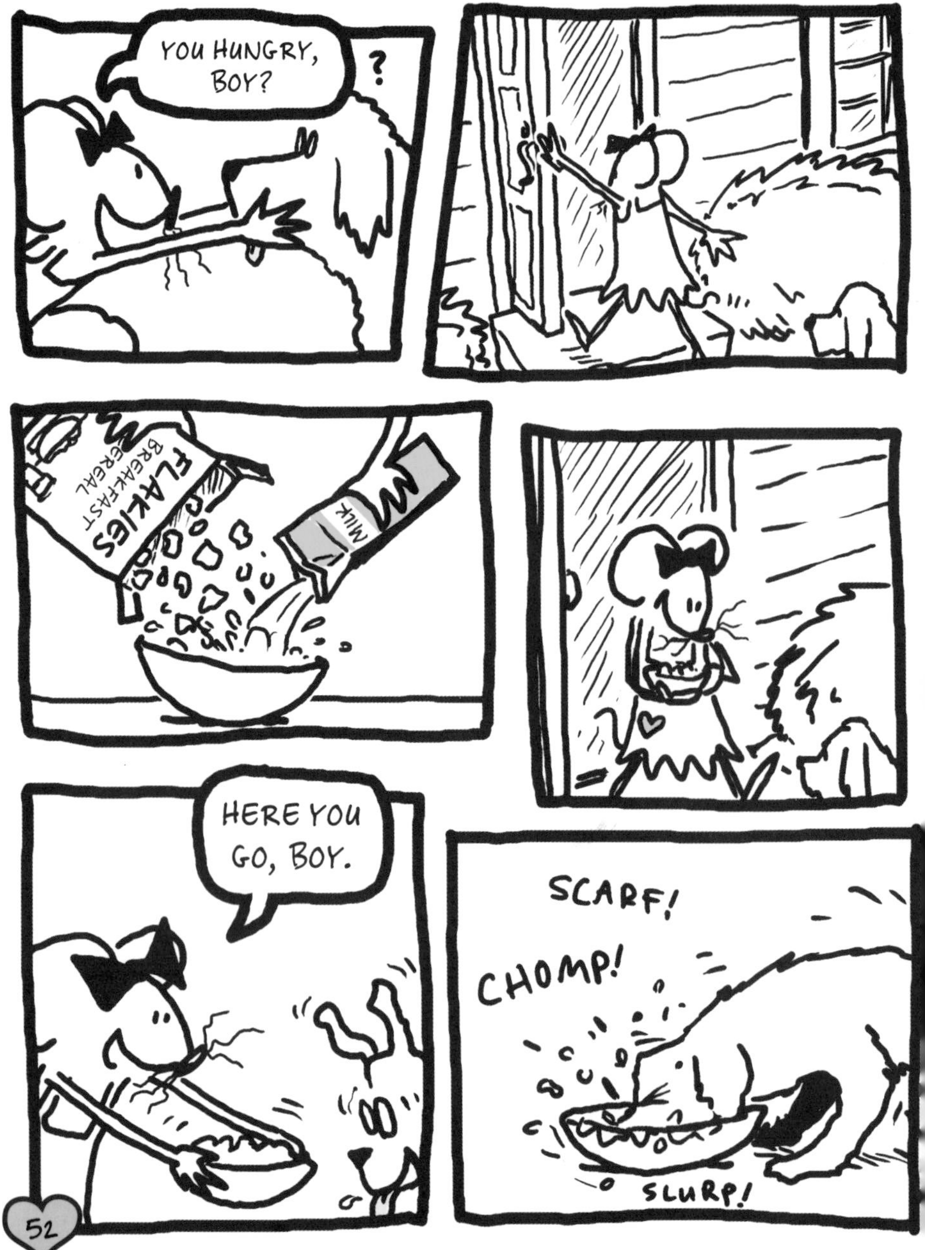
YOU HUNGRY, BOY?
?
FLAKIES BREAKFAST CEREAL
MILK
HERE YOU GO, BOY.
SCARF!
CHOMP!
SLURP!

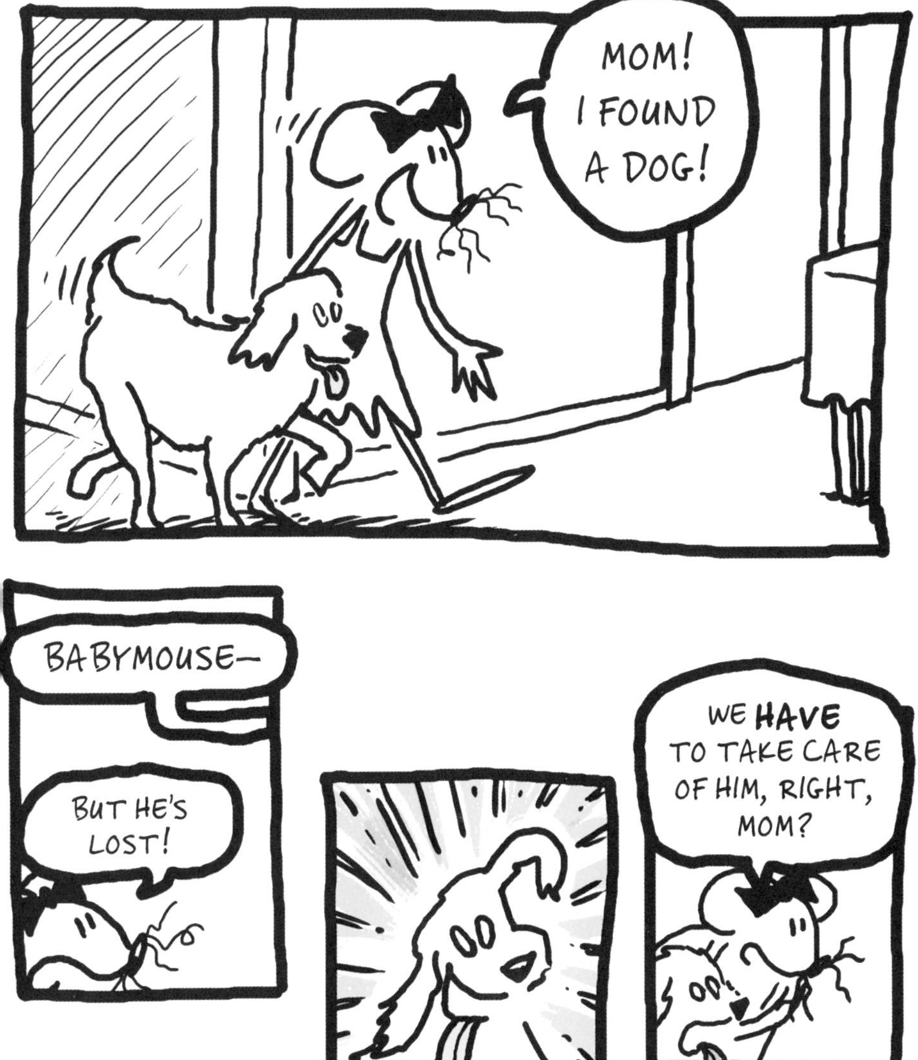
MOM! I FOUND A DOG!
BABYMOUSE—
BUT HE'S LOST!
WE **HAVE** TO TAKE CARE OF HIM, RIGHT, MOM?

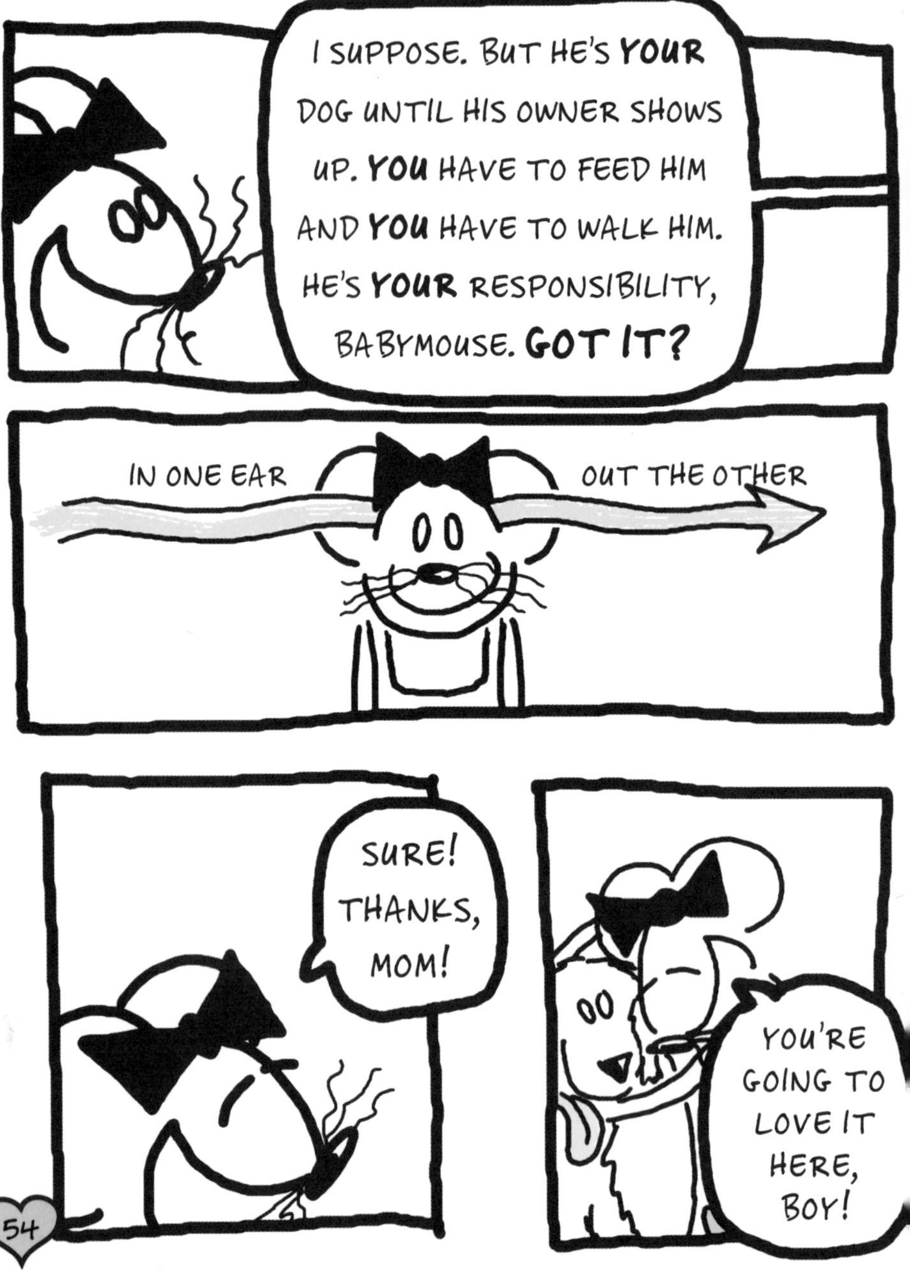
I SUPPOSE. BUT HE'S **YOUR** DOG UNTIL HIS OWNER SHOWS UP. **YOU** HAVE TO FEED HIM AND **YOU** HAVE TO WALK HIM. HE'S **YOUR** RESPONSIBILITY, BABYMOUSE. **GOT IT?**
IN ONE EAR
OUT THE OTHER
SURE! THANKS, MOM!
YOU'RE GOING TO LOVE IT HERE, BOY!

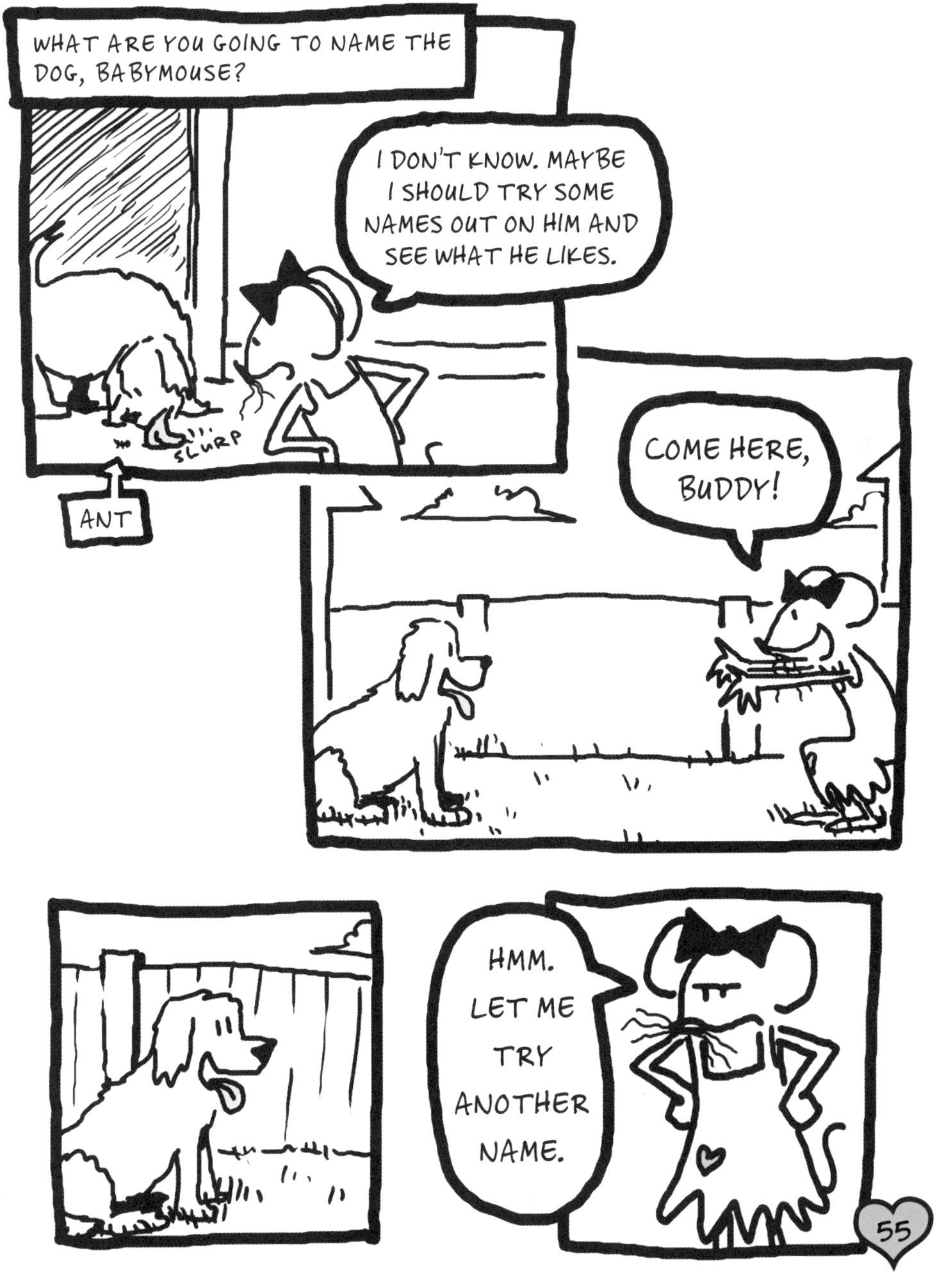
WHAT ARE YOU GOING TO NAME THE DOG, BABYMOUSE?
I DON'T KNOW. MAYBE I SHOULD TRY SOME NAMES OUT ON HIM AND SEE WHAT HE LIKES.
SLURP
ANT
COME HERE, BUDDY!
HMM. LET ME TRY ANOTHER NAME.

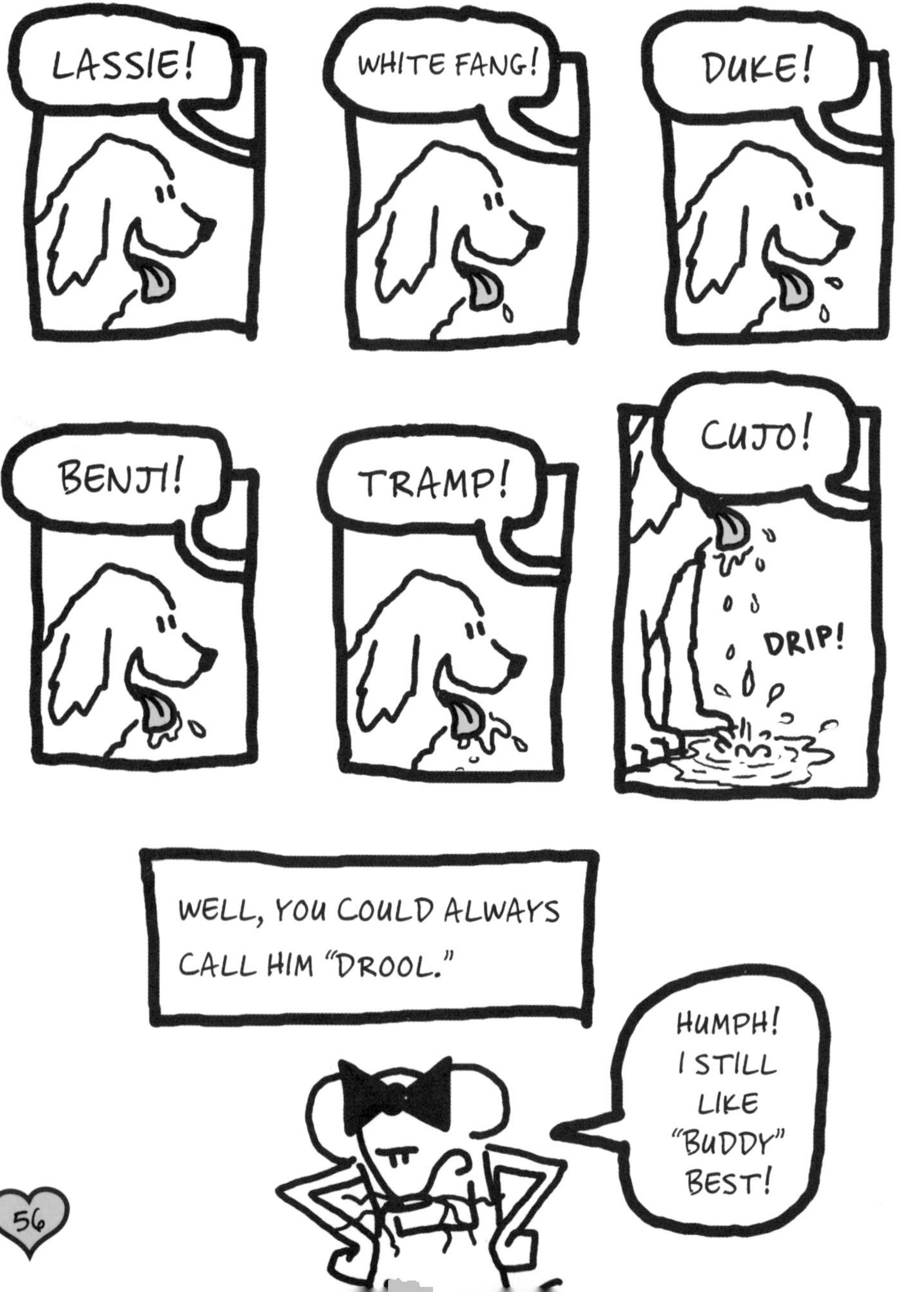
LASSIE!
WHITE FANG!
DUKE!
BENJI!
TRAMP!
CUJO!
DRIP!
WELL, YOU COULD ALWAYS CALL HIM "DROOL."
HUMPH! I STILL LIKE "BUDDY" BEST!

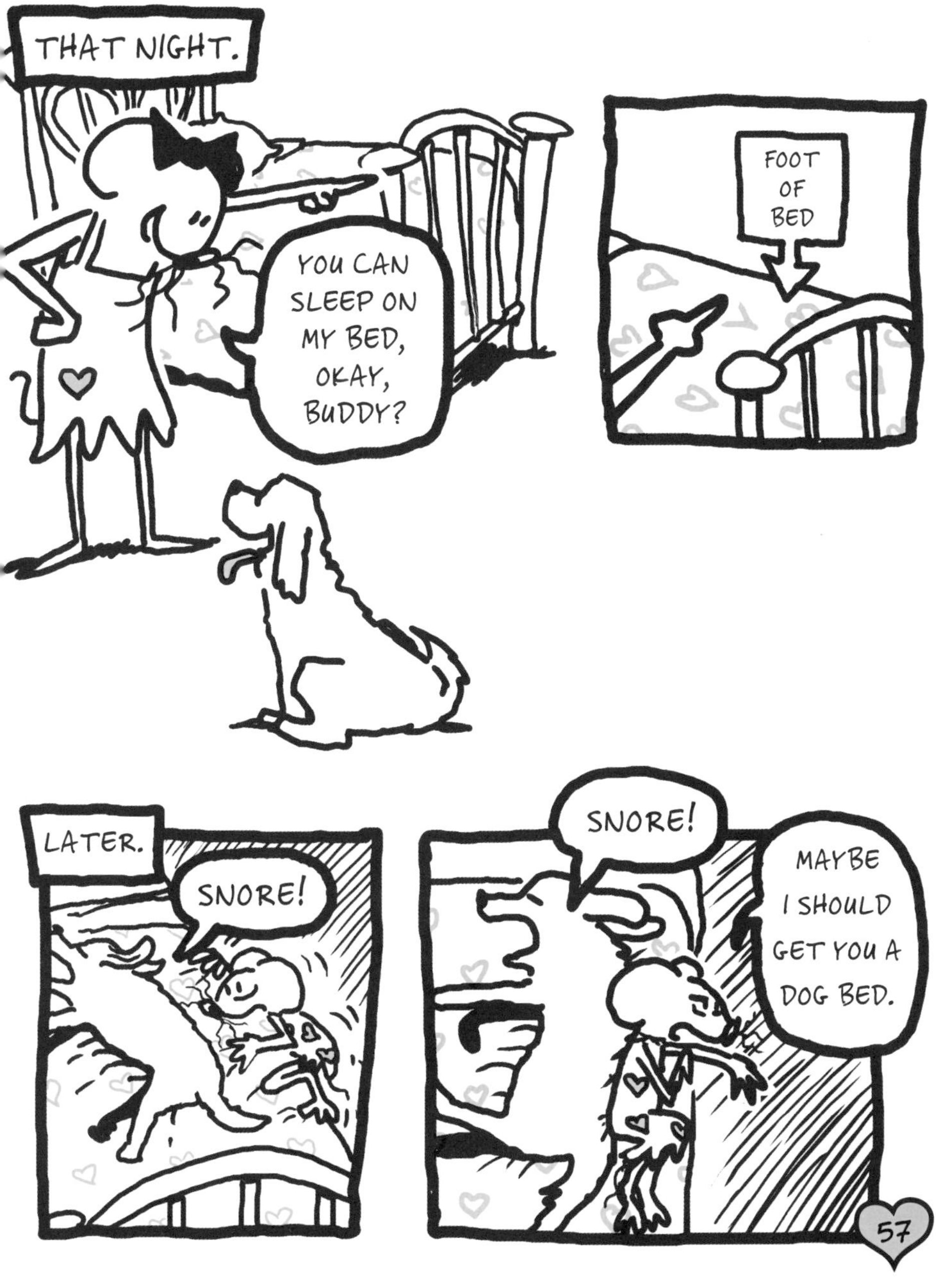
THAT NIGHT.
YOU CAN SLEEP ON MY BED, OKAY, BUDDY?
FOOT OF BED
LATER.
SNORE!
SNORE!
MAYBE I SHOULD GET YOU A DOG BED.

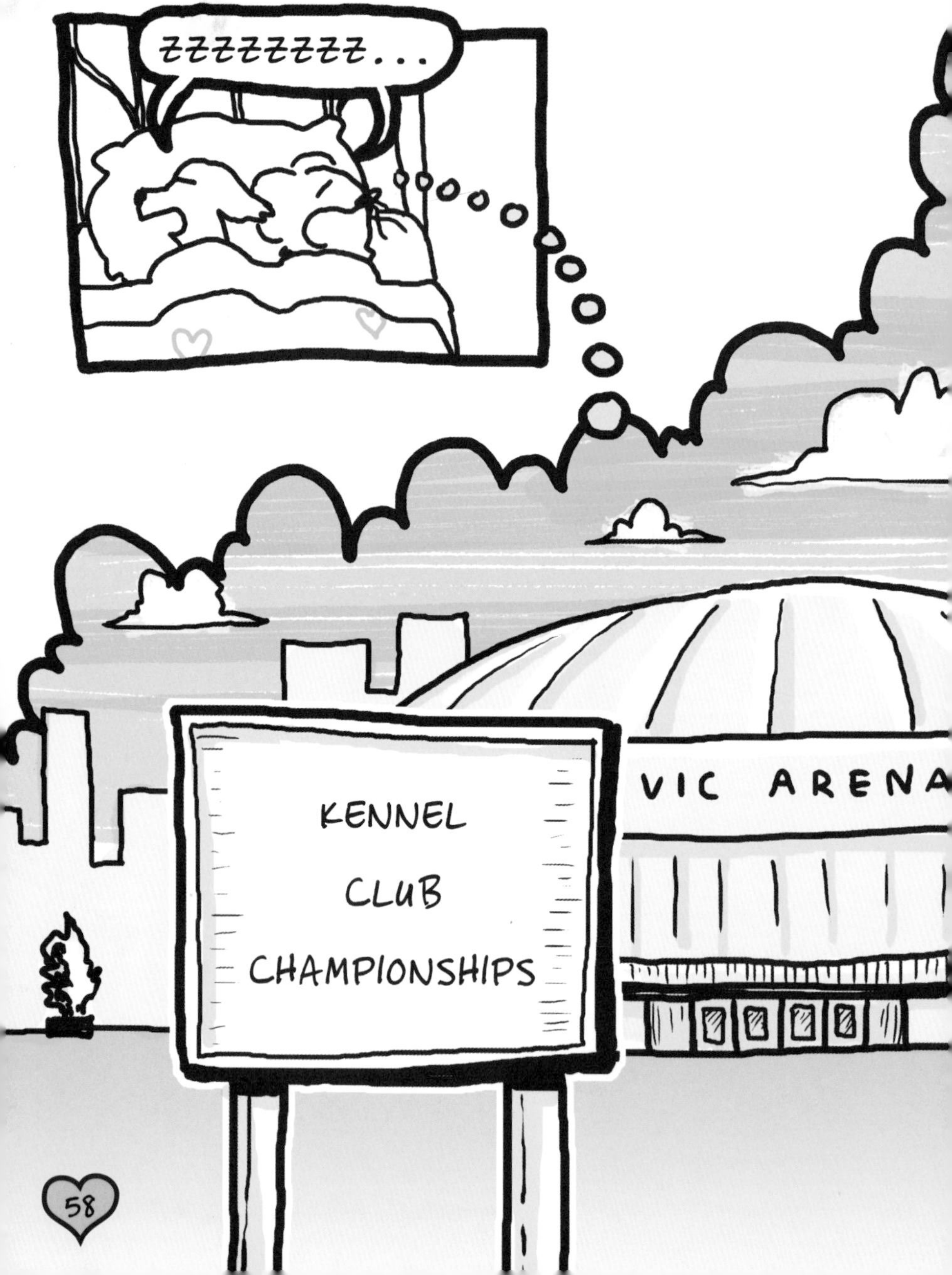
ZZZZZZZZZ...
KENNEL CLUB CHAMPIONSHIPS
VIC ARENA

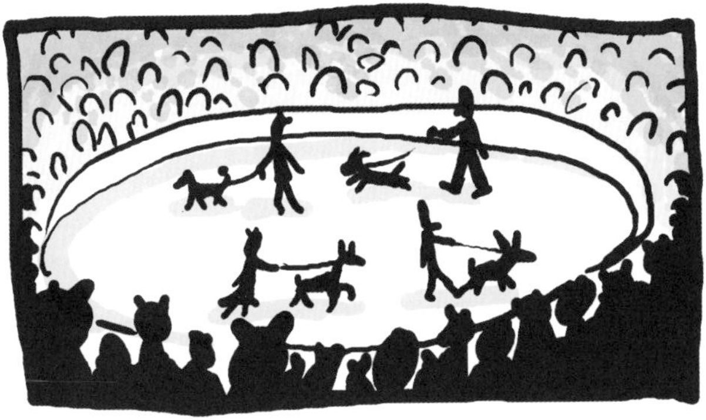

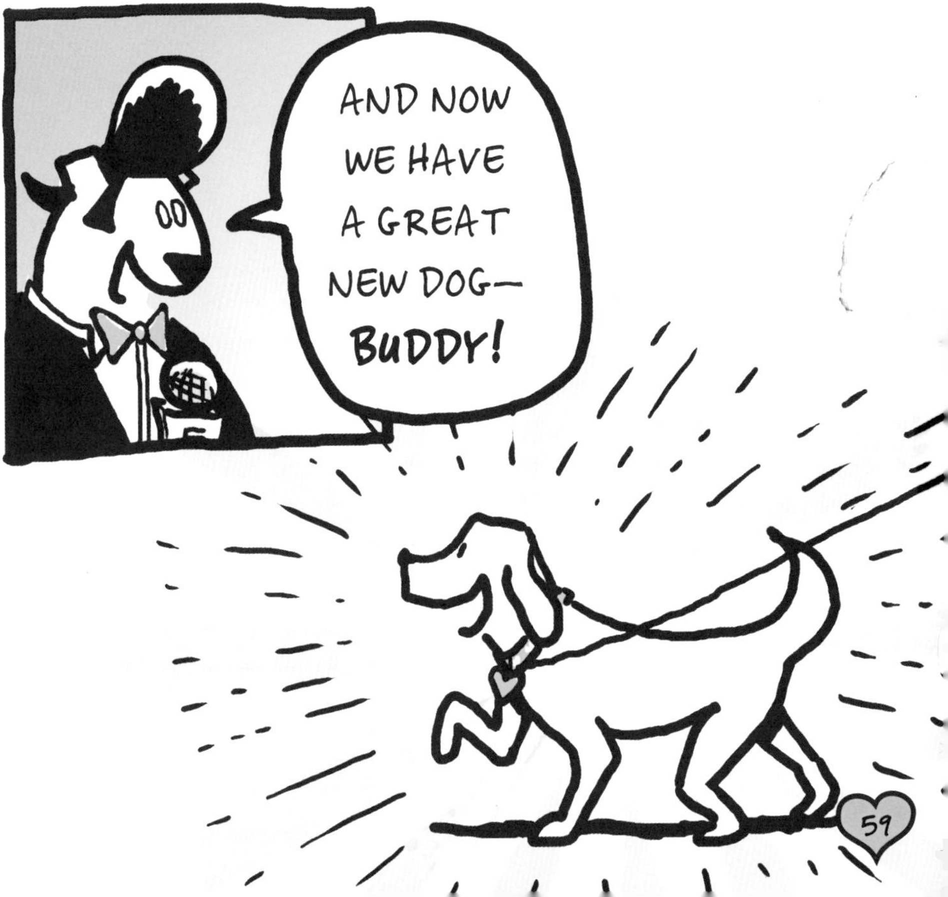
AND NOW WE HAVE A GREAT NEW DOG— BUDDY!

BUDDY IS A PUREBRED LAB-CHOW-TERRIER-HOUND-BULLDOG MIX.

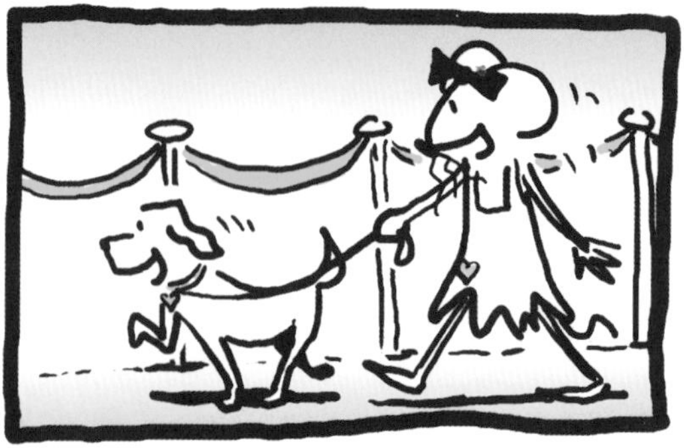

BUDDY'S OWNER, BABYMOUSE, HAS BEEN WORKING WITH HIM FOR SOME TIME NOW.

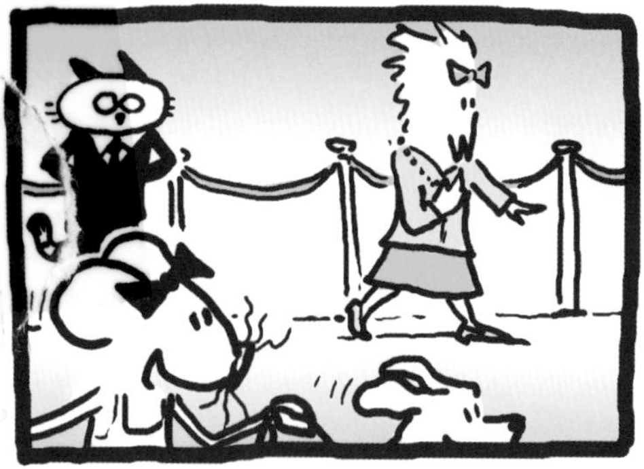

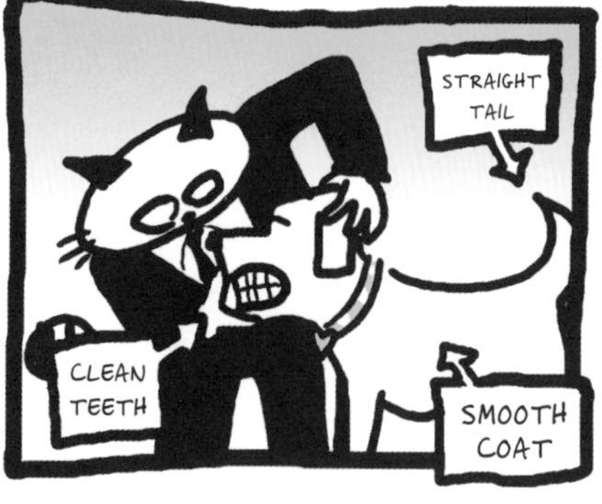
STRAIGHT TAIL
CLEAN TEETH
SMOOTH COAT

LOOKS LIKE THE JUDGES ARE TALLYING THE SCORES...

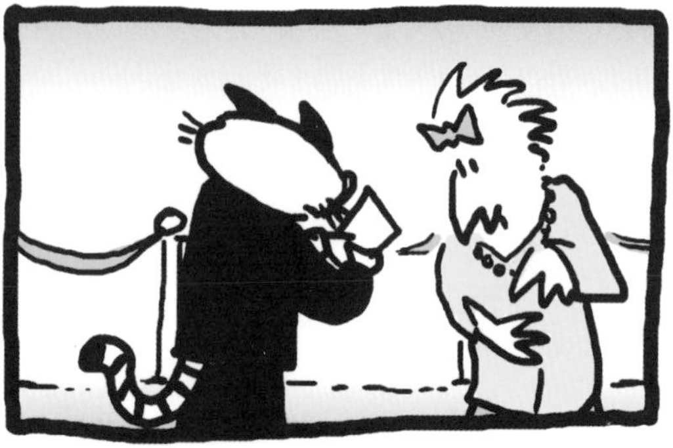

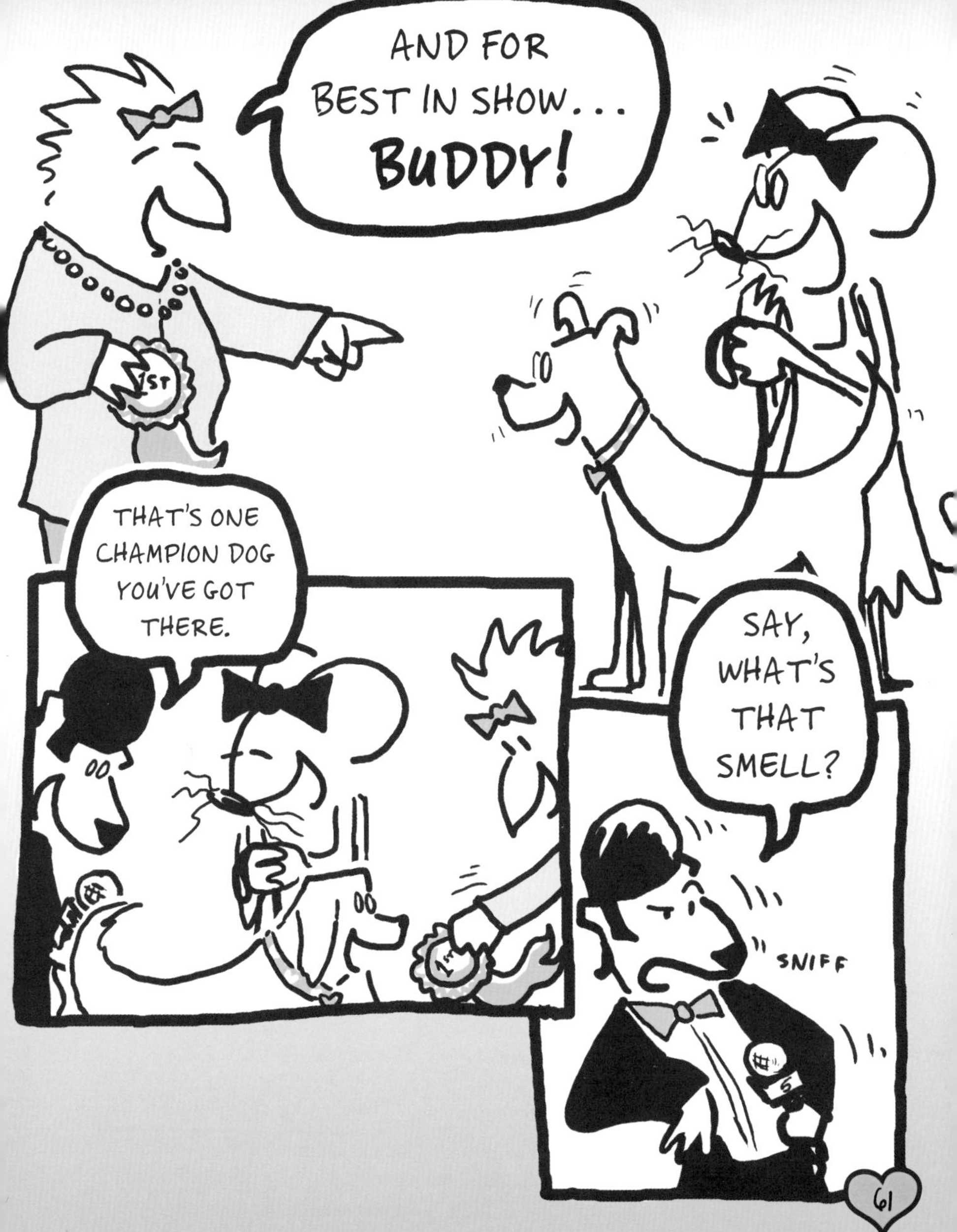

AND FOR BEST IN SHOW... BUDDY!
THAT'S ONE CHAMPION DOG YOU'VE GOT THERE.
SAY, WHAT'S THAT SMELL?
SNIFF

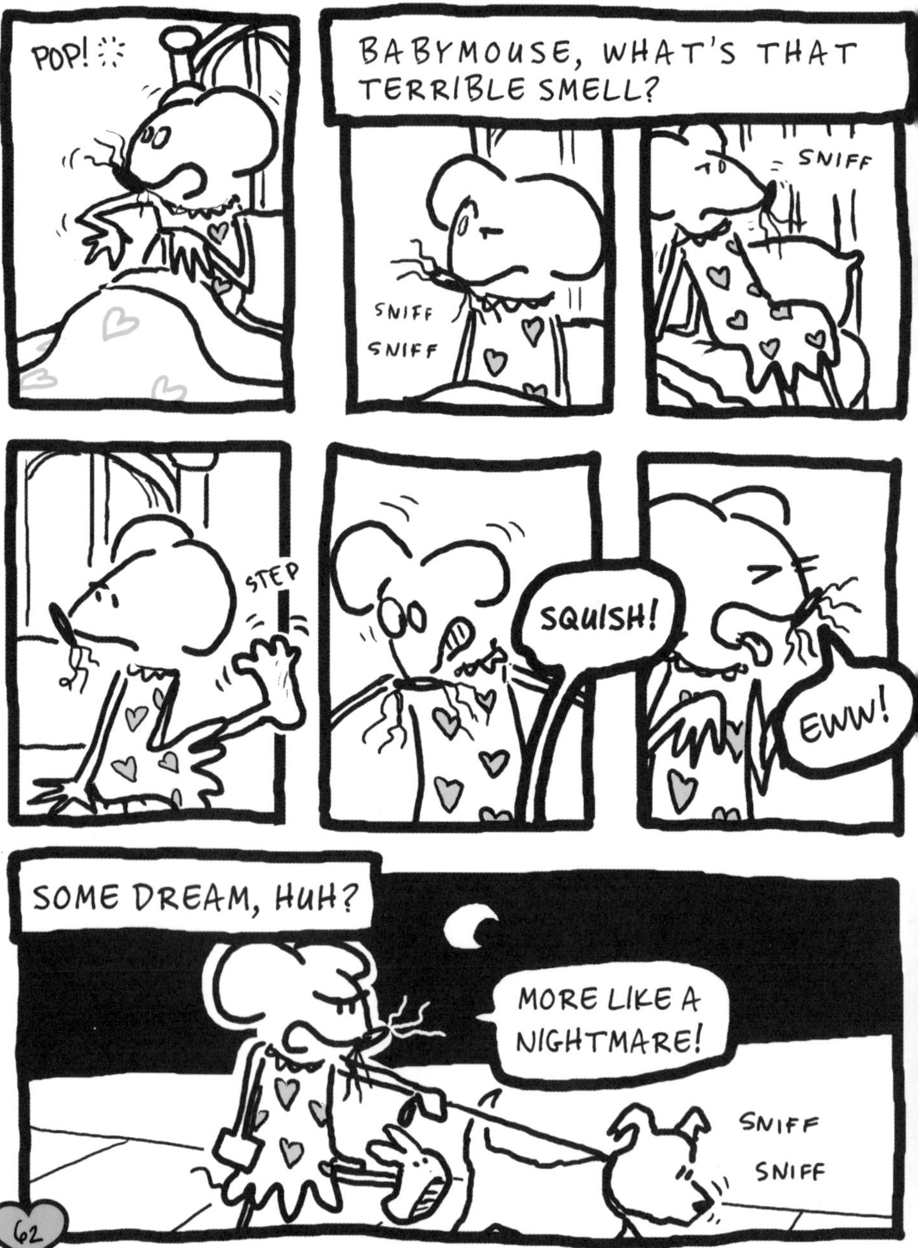
POP!
BABYMOUSE, WHAT'S THAT TERRIBLE SMELL?
SNIFF
SNIFF
SNIFF
STEP
SQUISH!
EWW!
SOME DREAM, HUH?
MORE LIKE A NIGHTMARE!
SNIFF
SNIFF

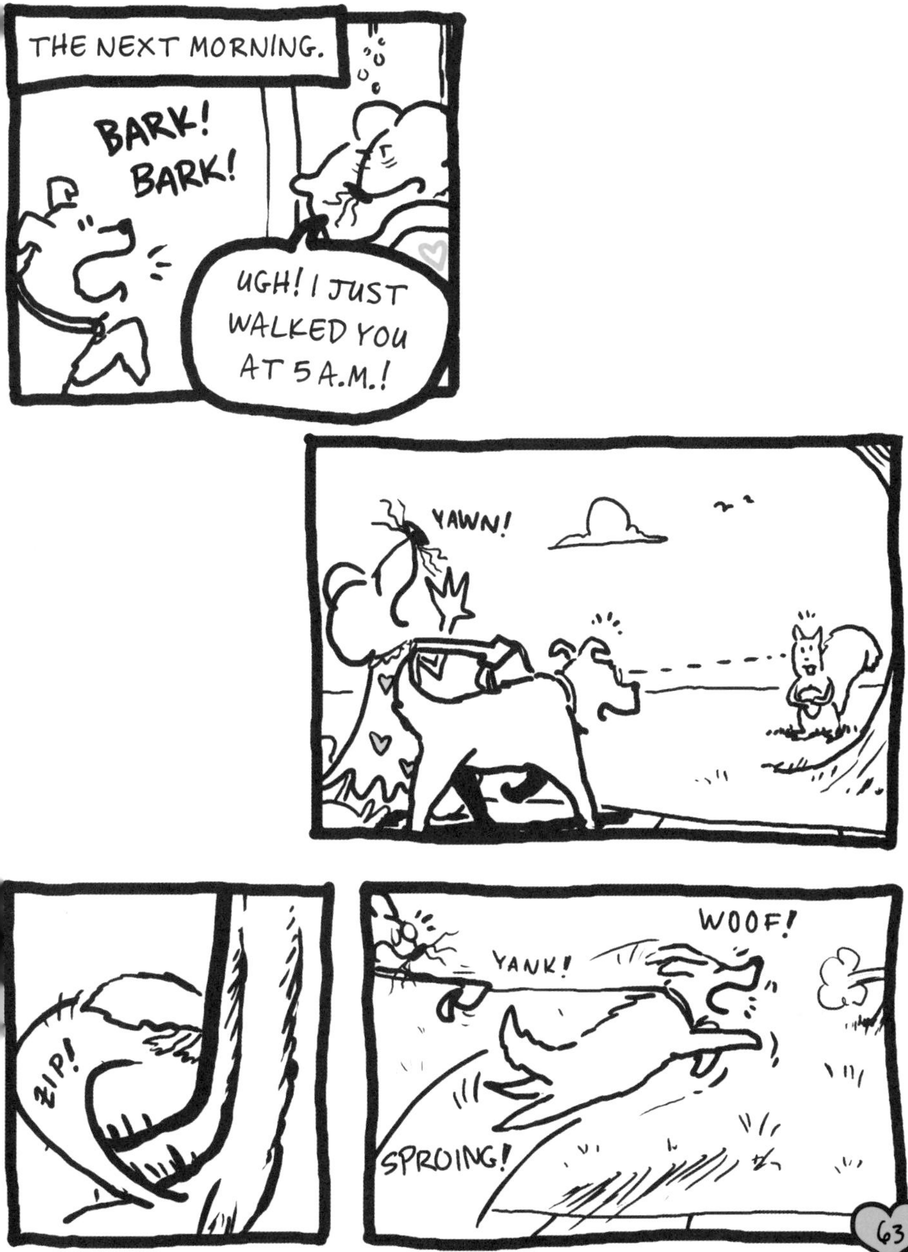
THE NEXT MORNING.
BARK! BARK!
UGH! I JUST WALKED YOU AT 5 A.M.!
YAWN!
ZIP!
WOOF!
YANK!
SPROING!

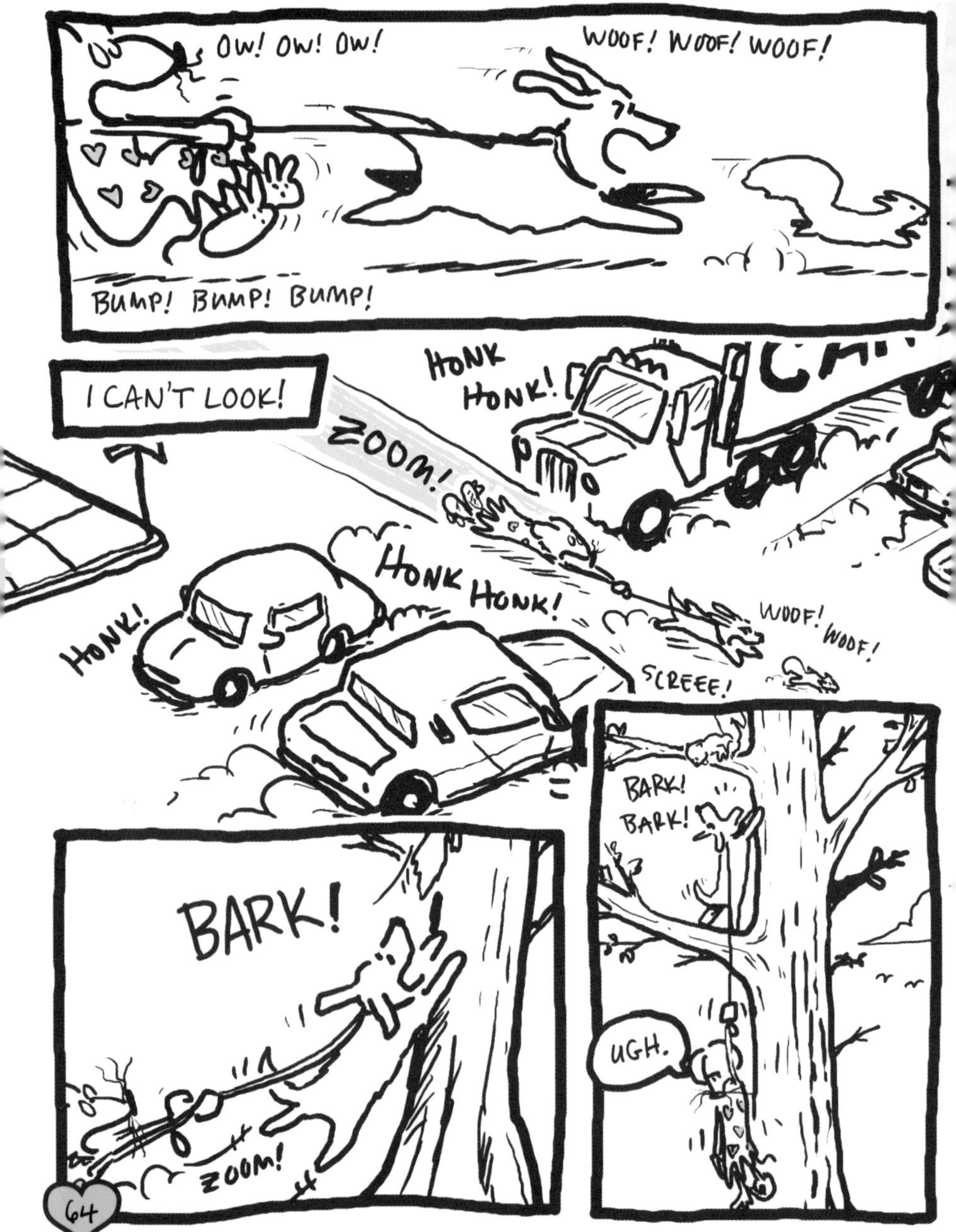
OW! OW! OW!
WOOF! WOOF! WOOF!
BUMP! BUMP! BUMP!
I CAN'T LOOK!
HONK HONK!
ZOOM!
HONK HONK!
HONK!
WOOF! WOOF!
SCREEE!
BARK!
ZOOM!
BARK! BARK!
UGH.

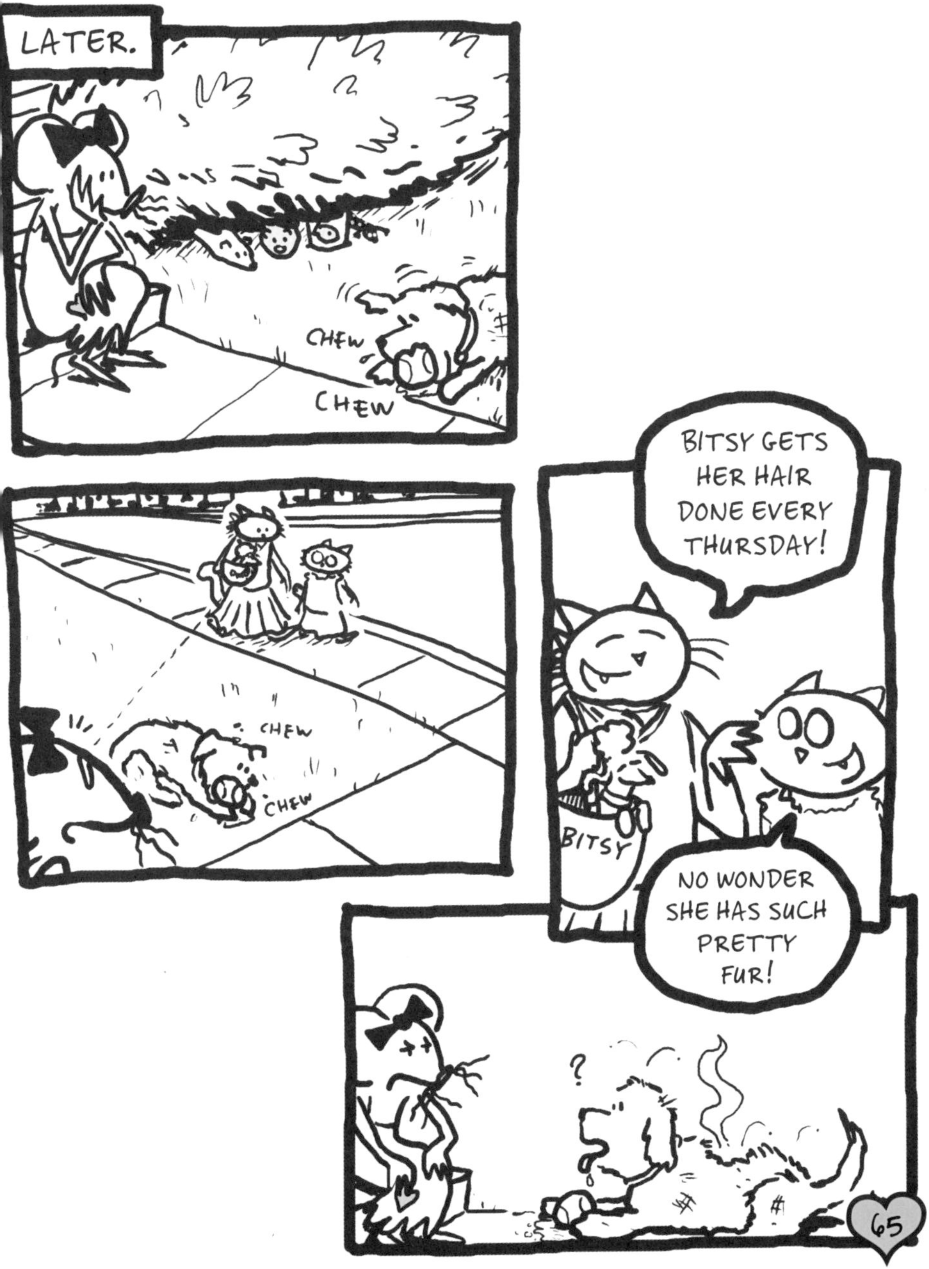
LATER.
CHEW
CHEW
CHEW
CHEW
BITSY GETS HER HAIR DONE EVERY THURSDAY!
BITSY
NO WONDER SHE HAS SUCH PRETTY FUR!
?

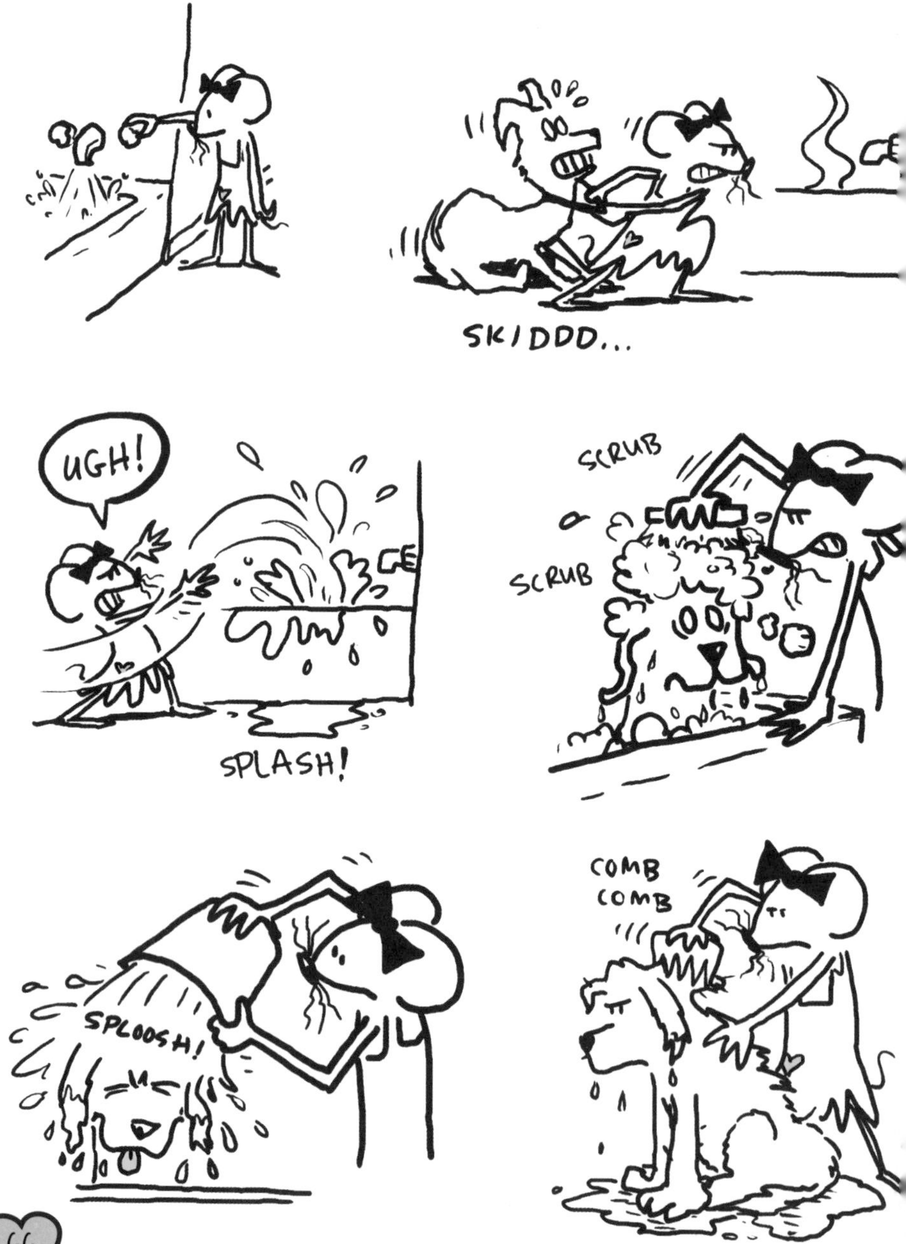
SKIDDD...
UGH!
SPLASH!
SCRUB
SCRUB
SPLOOSH!
COMB
COMB

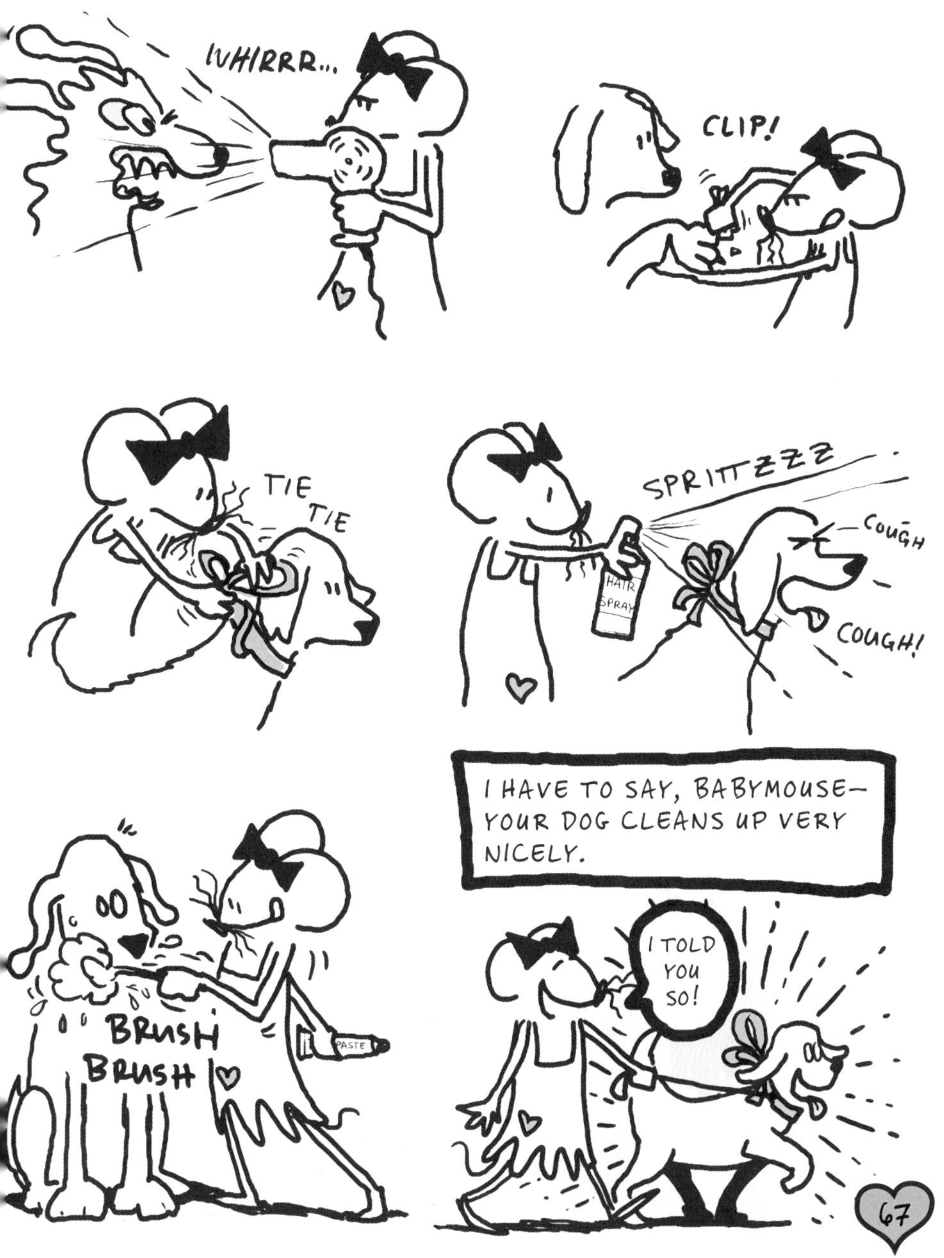
WHIRRR...
CLIP!
TIE
TIE
SPRITTZZZ
HAIR SPRAY
COUGH
COUGH!
BRUSH
BRUSH
PASTE
I HAVE TO SAY, BABYMOUSE—YOUR DOG CLEANS UP VERY NICELY.
I TOLD YOU SO!

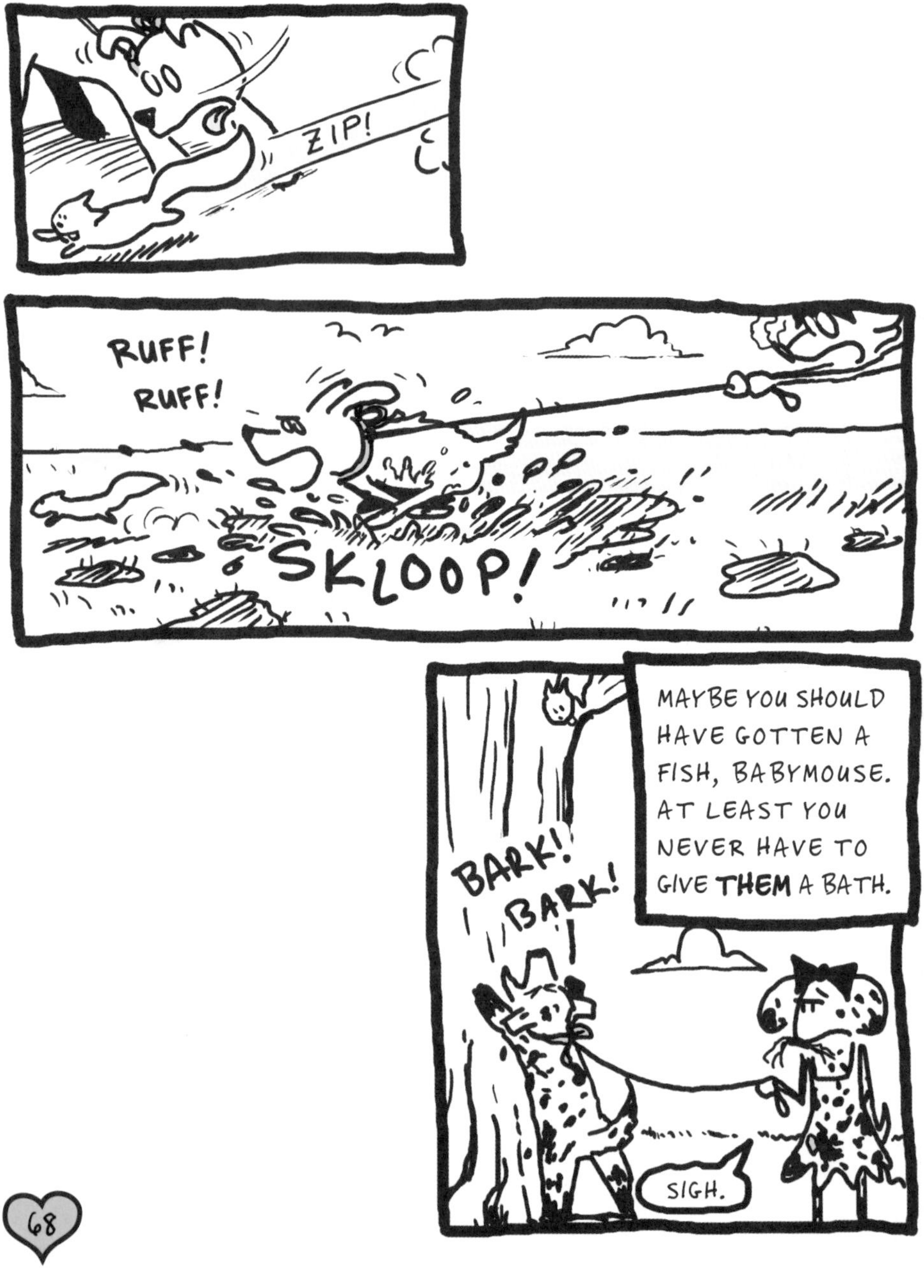
ZIP!
RUFF!
RUFF!
SKLOOP!
MAYBE YOU SHOULD HAVE GOTTEN A FISH, BABYMOUSE. AT LEAST YOU NEVER HAVE TO GIVE THEM A BATH.
BARK!
BARK!
SIGH.

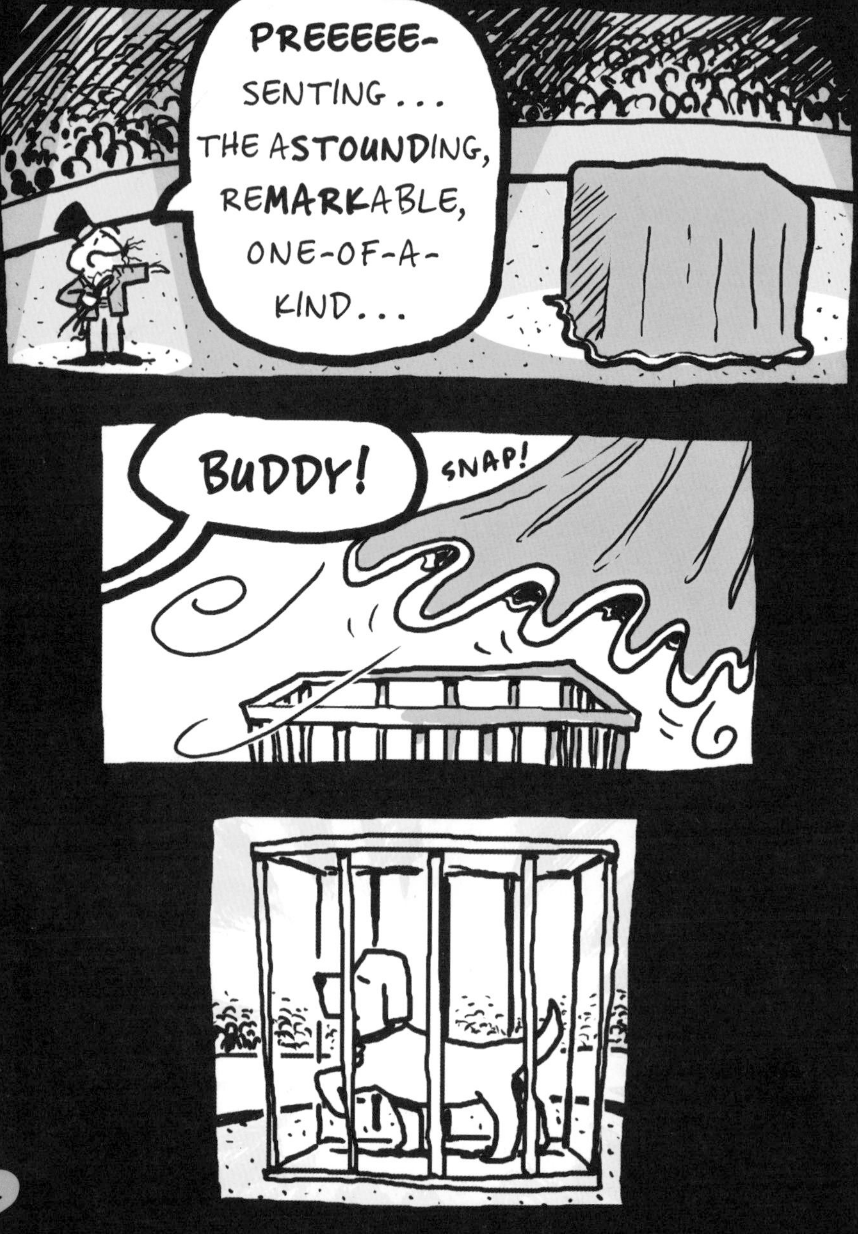
PREEEEE-SENTING . . . THE ASTOUNDING, REMARKABLE, ONE-OF-A-KIND . . .
BUDDY!
SNAP!

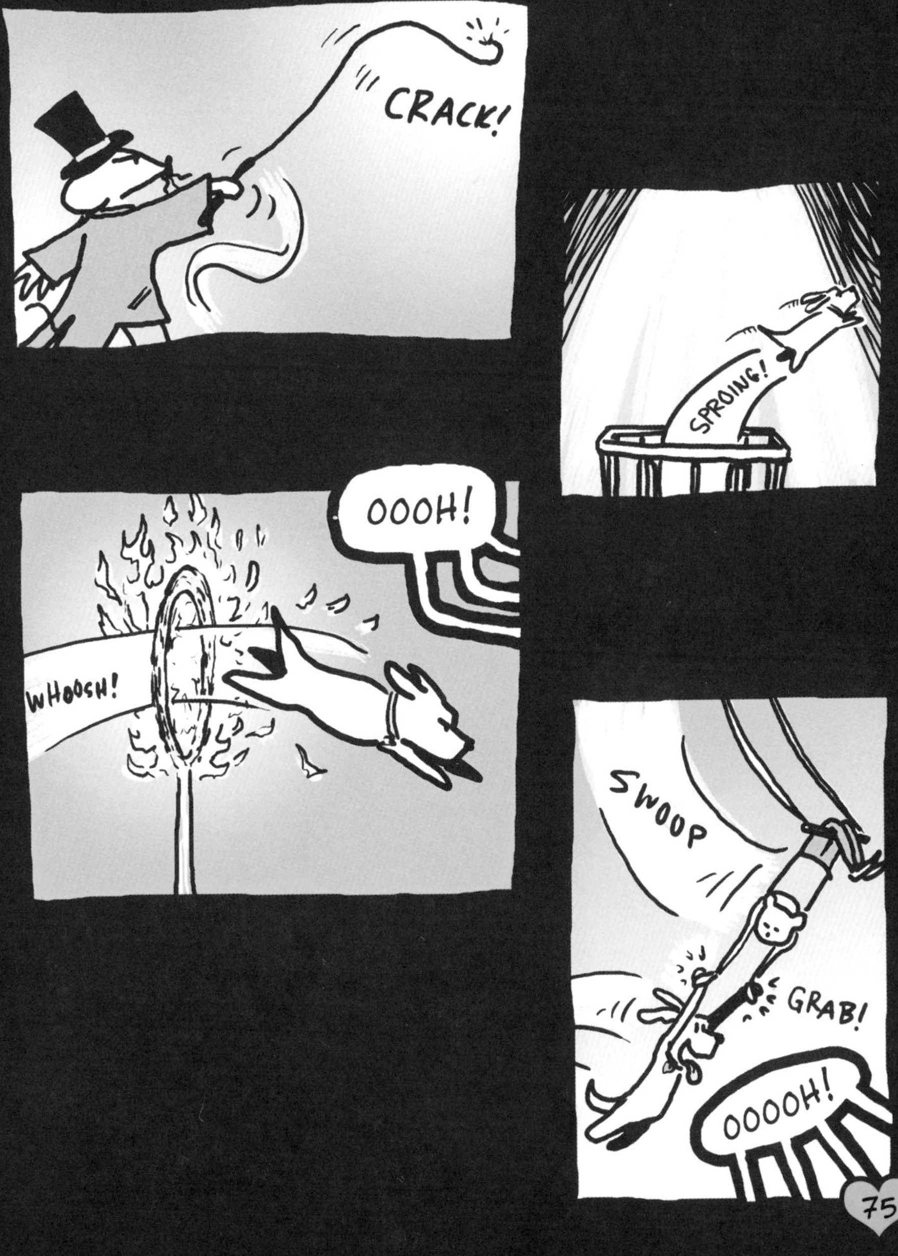
CRACK!
SPROING!
WHOOSH!
OOOH!
SWOOP
GRAB!
OOOOH!

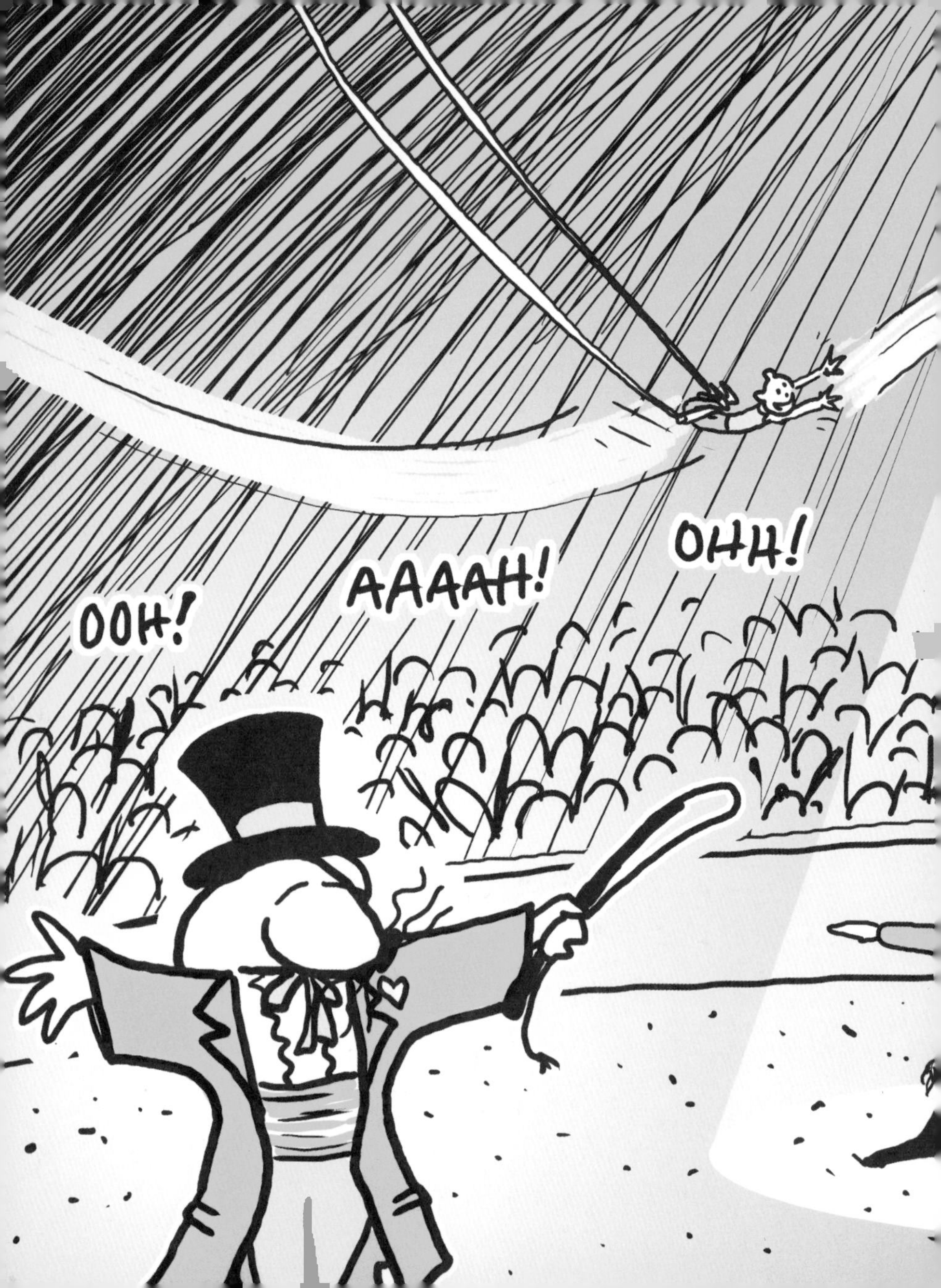
OOH!
AAAAH!
OHH!

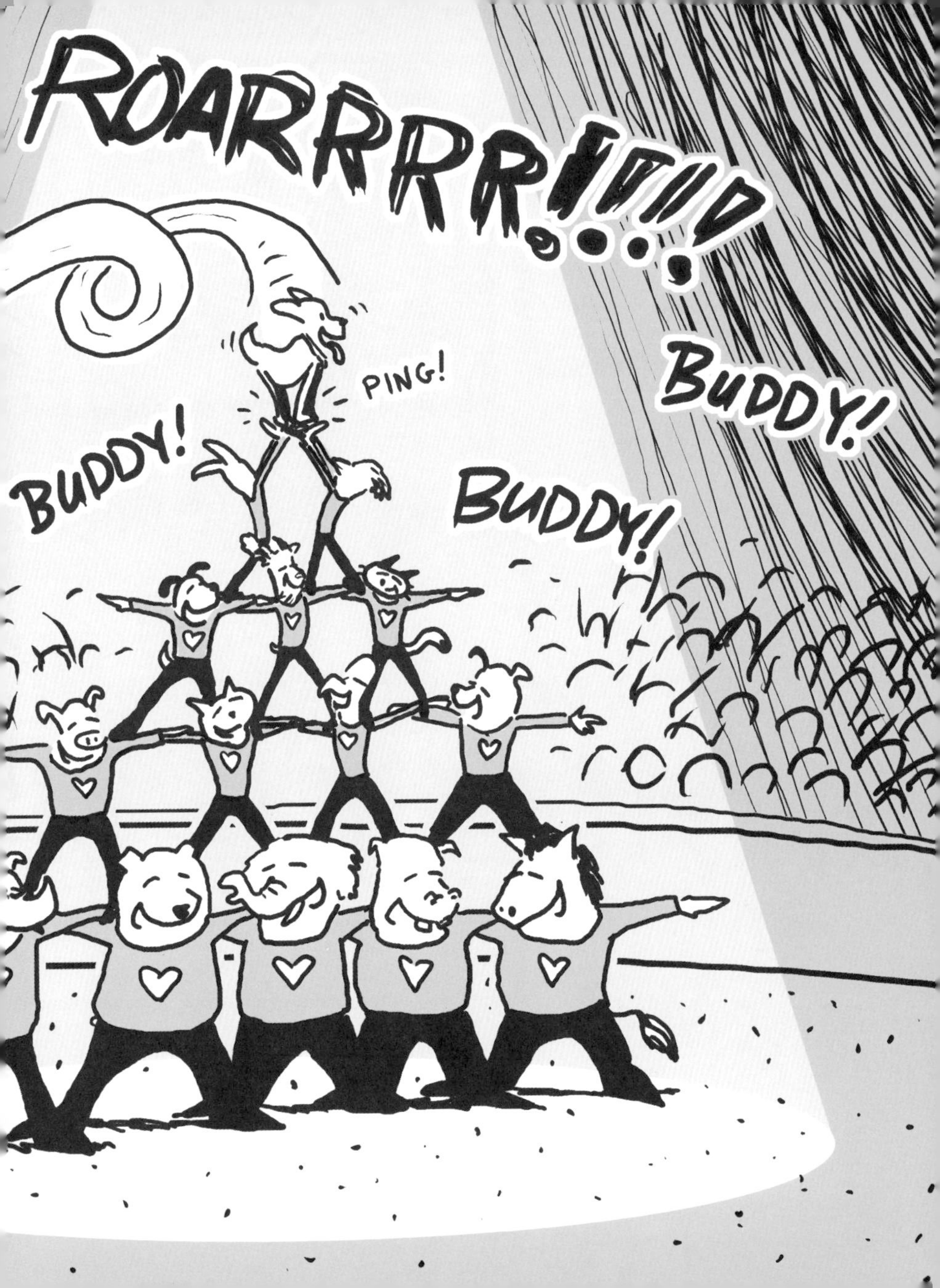
ROARRRRR!!!!!
PING!
BUDDY!
BUDDY!
BUDDY!

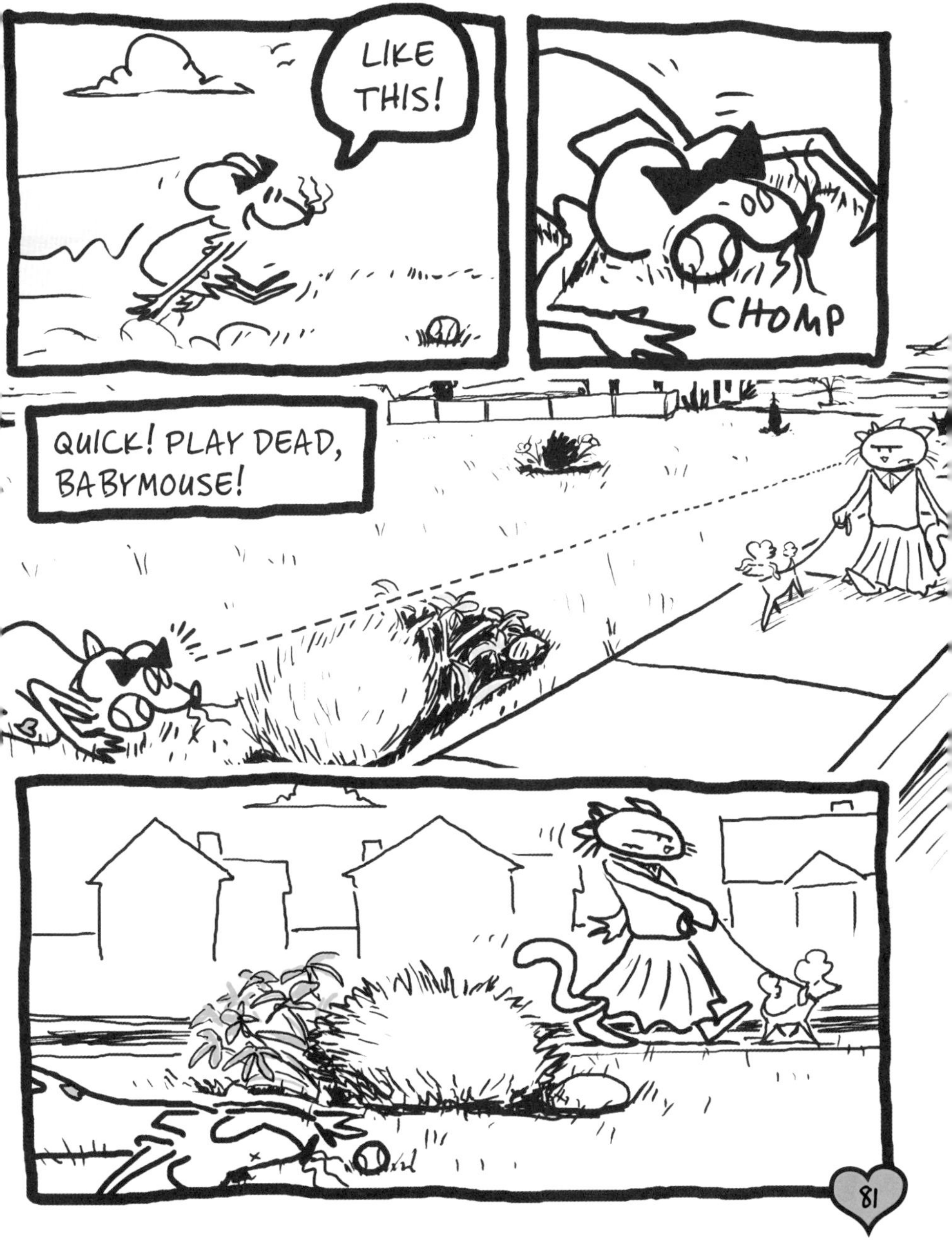
LIKE THIS!
CHOMP
QUICK! PLAY DEAD, BABYMOUSE!

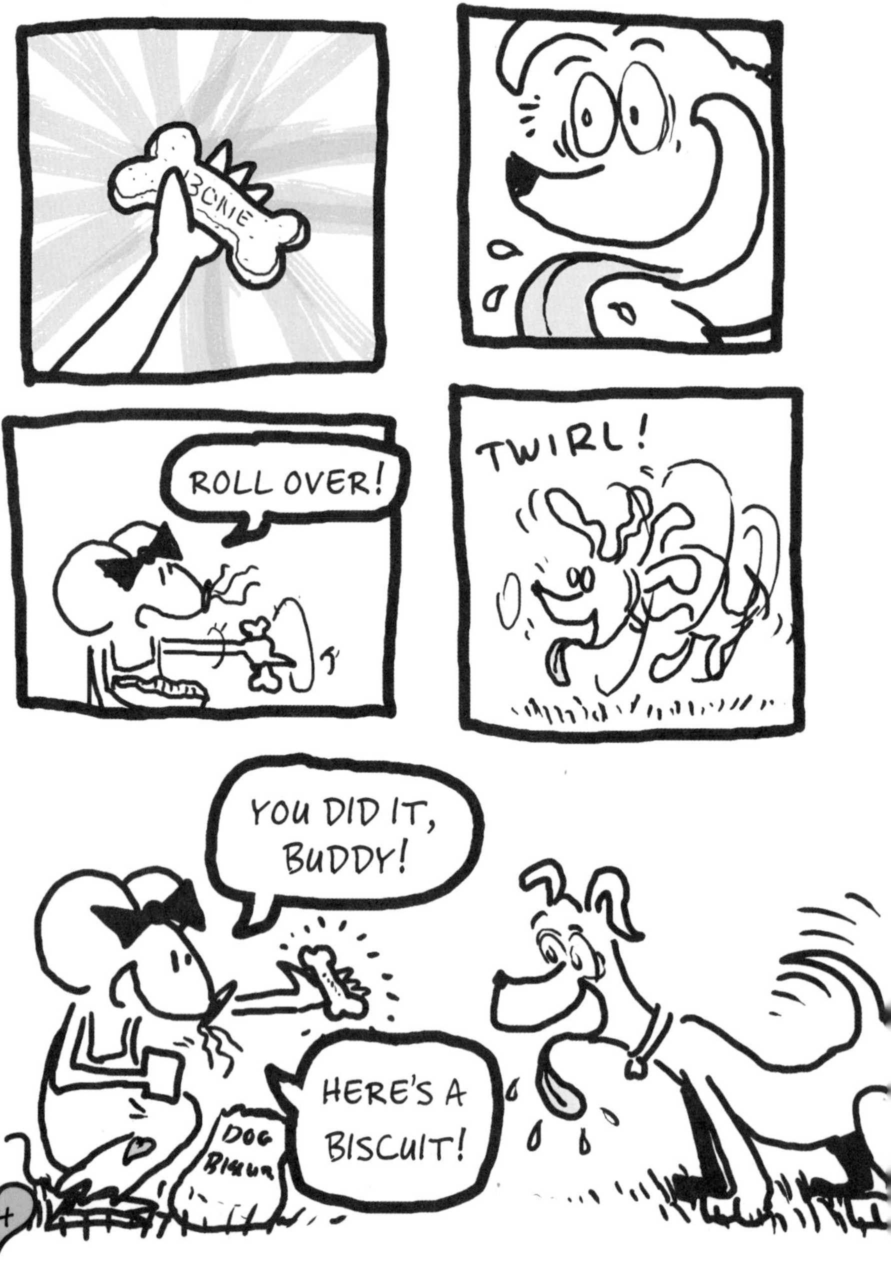
BONE
ROLL OVER!
TWIRL!
YOU DID IT, BUDDY!
HERE'S A BISCUIT!
DOG

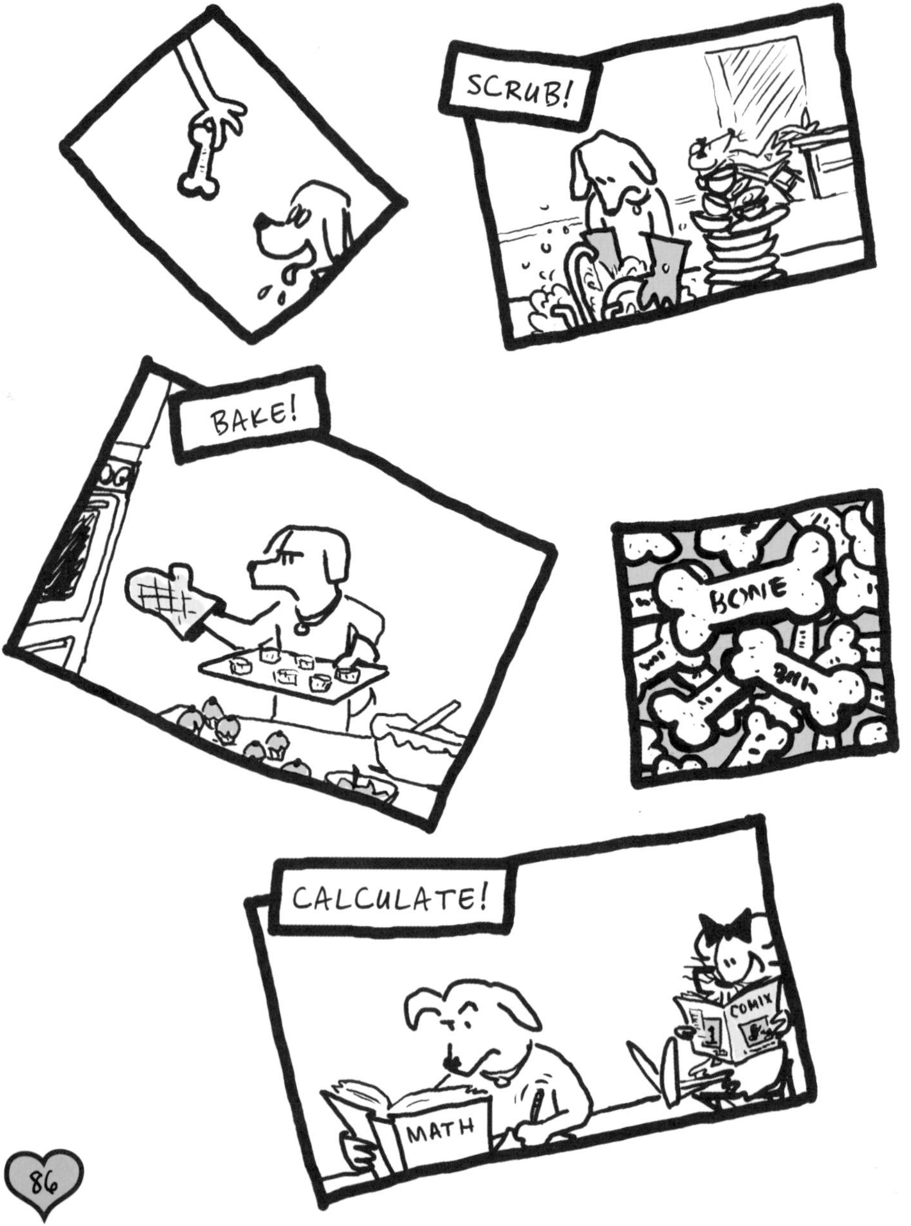
SCRUB!
BAKE!
BONE
CALCULATE!
COMIX
MATH

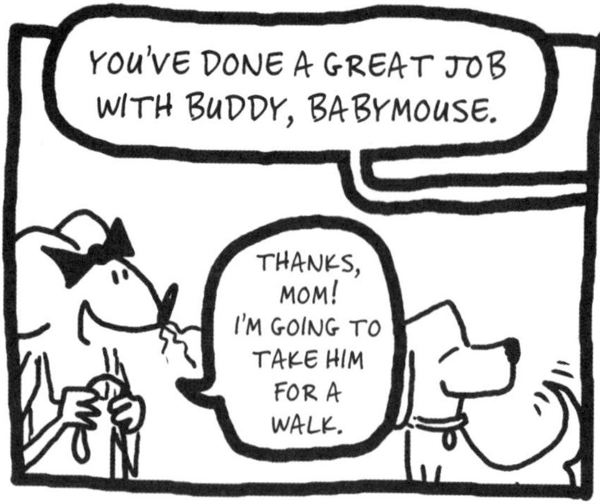
YOU'VE DONE A GREAT JOB WITH BUDDY, BABYMOUSE.
THANKS, MOM! I'M GOING TO TAKE HIM FOR A WALK.
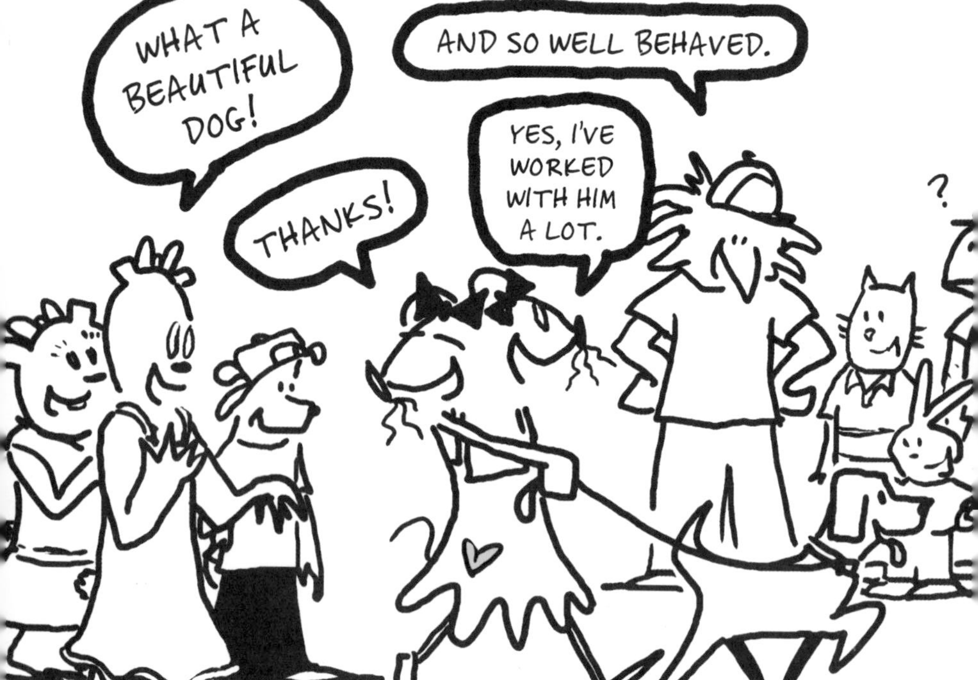
WHAT A BEAUTIFUL DOG!
THANKS!
AND SO WELL BEHAVED.
YES, I'VE WORKED WITH HIM A LOT.
?

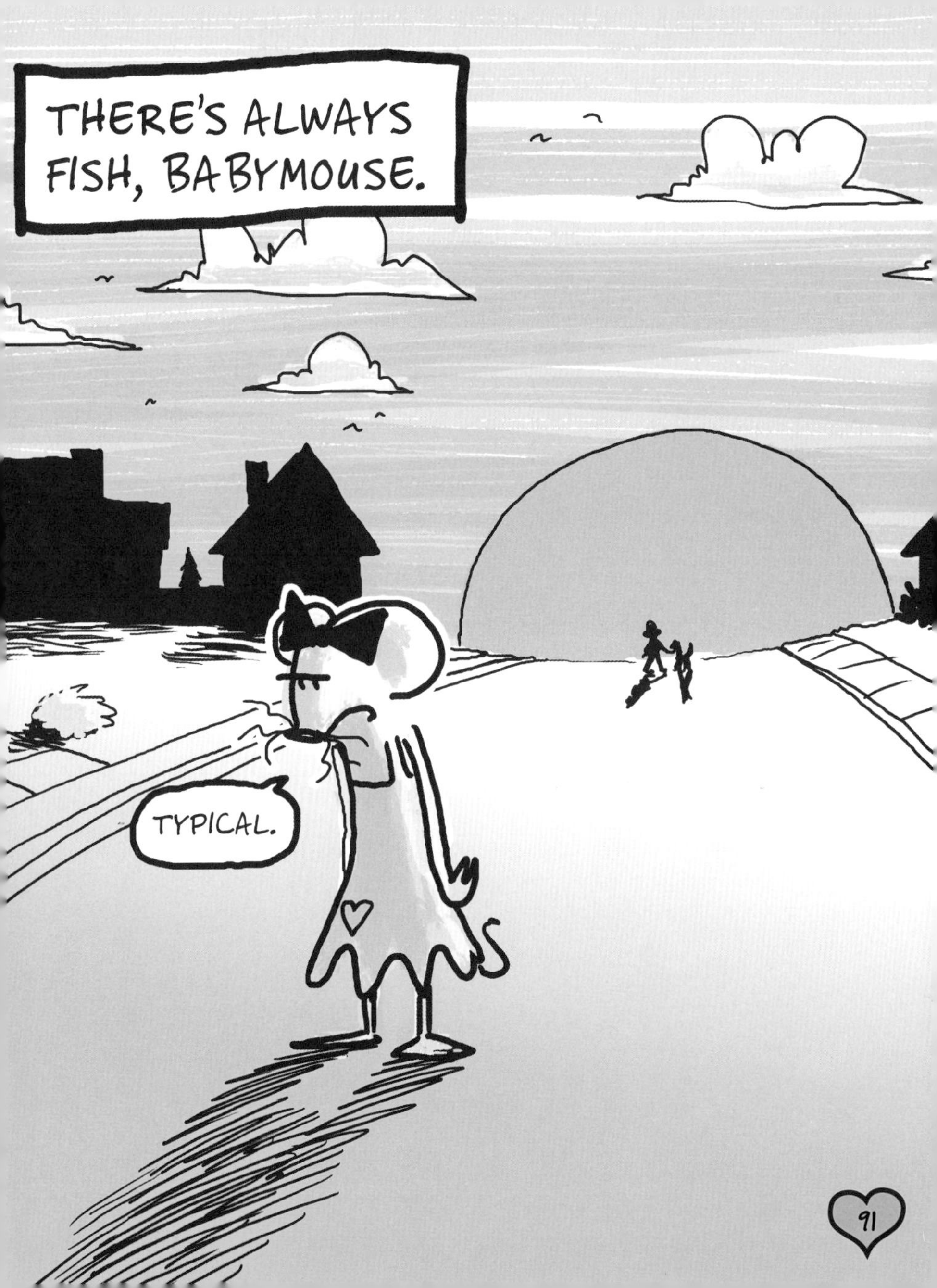
THERE'S ALWAYS FISH, BABYMOUSE.
TYPICAL.